Frederik Pohl

The Age of the Pussyfoot

PANTHER
GRANADA PUBLISHING
London Toronto Sydney New York

Published by Granada Publishing Limited
in Panther Books 1979

ISBN 0 586 04830 8

First published in Great Britain by Victor
Gollancz Ltd 1970
Copyright © Frederik Pohl 1969

The Age of the Pussyfoot previously appeared in a shorter
version in Galaxy Magazine 1965–6
Copyright © Galaxy Publishing Corporation 1965, 1966

Granada Publishing Limited
Frogmore, St Albans, Herts AL2 2NF
and
3 Upper James Street, London W1R 4BP
866 United Nations Plaza, New York, NY 10017, USA
117 York Street, Sydney, NSW 2000, Australia
100 Skyway Avenue, Rexdale, Ontario, M9W 3A6, Canada
PO Box 84165, Greenside, 2034 Johannesburg, South Africa
CML Centre, Queen & Wyndham, Auckland 1, New Zealand

Set, printed and bound in Great Britain by
Cox & Wyman Ltd, Reading
Set in Intertype Times

Granada ®
Granada Publishing ®

Born in New York in 1919, Frederik Pohl's first contribution to an SF publication was a poem, 'Elegy to a Dead Planet: Luna', in *Amazing* (1937). He edited *Astonishing* and *Super Science Stories* 1940–41, and *Star Science Fiction Stories* for Ballantine Books, 1953–59. He then edited *Galaxy* and *If* for several years. His celebrated partnership with C. M. Kornbluth produced *The Space Merchants* (1953), one of the major SF classics of the 50s, depicting an over-populated world dedicated completely to consumerism and dominated by brain-washing advertising. Kornbluth died in 1958, but Pohl continued writing and is established as one of the classic writers of hard-core science fiction. His most recent Nebula Award-winning novel is *Man Plus*, also published in Panther.

Also by Frederik Pohl

The Space Merchants (with C. M. Kornbluth)
Search the Sky (with C. M. Kornbluth)
Gladiator-at-Law (with C. M. Kornbluth)
Wolfbane (with C. M. Kornbluth)
The Reefs of Space (with Jack Williamson)
Starchild (with Jack Williamson)
Rogue Star (with Jack Williamson)

Slave Ship
A Plague of Pythons
*Drunkard's Walk**
*Man Plus**

Short Stories
Alternating Currents
The Case Against Tomorrow
Tomorrow Times Seven
Turn Left at Thursday
The Abominable Earthman
*The Gold at the Starbow's End**
The Wonder Effect (with C. M. Kornbluth)*
*Survival Kit**
*The Man Who Ate the World**

*Available in Panther Science Fiction

Foreword

I have two conflicting opinions. One is that any story should stand on its own feet – which means that, generally speaking, anything a writer has to say about his own story is better left unsaid. If it's worth saying, why didn't he say it in the story itself?

The other opinion, however, is equally firmly fixed in my mind, and at this moment it is in direct conflict with the first. That is, I think that more people should read science fiction than appear to be willing to do so; and I think the reason for this is that many people regard it as crazy, fantastic stuff with no basis in the real world and no relevance to their own lives.

I would like to hope that some people will read this book who normally don't read science fiction. If you are one of them, and if you begin to feel like those many others mentioned above, please pause in your reading and go on to look at the author's note included in the back of the book.

It seems to me that science fiction can have relevance to the real world and, yes, to your own life. And some of my reasons for thinking so are set forth there . . .

The Age of the Pussyfoot

ONE

Over everyone in the room, or perhaps it was a park, the lighting cast shapes and symbols of color. The girl in the filmy gown had at one moment glittering pink eyes and, at the next, an aura of silvery hair. The man next to Forrester had golden skin and a mask of shadow. Wisps of odor drifted past him, rosebuds following sage. There were snatches of a crystalline, far-off music.

'I'm rich!' he yelled. 'And alive!'

No one seemed to mind. Forrester plucked one of the colorless grapes Hara had recommended to him, rose, patted the girl in the filmy dress, and walked unsteadily down to the pool where the revelers splashed and swam in a naked tangle. In spite of the long postrevival indoctrination that had given him so many new things and removed so much trash that was old, Forrester had not lost the habit of being a little dirty-minded, and he was interested in the nakedness.

'It's Forrester the rich man!' one of them shouted. Forrester smiled and waved. A girl cried, 'Sing him a song! A song!' And they all splashed at him and sang:

Oh, he died and he died and he died
(SPLASH!)
And he cried and he cried and he cried
(SPLASH!)
With his rages and his cholers he's a puzzle to the schol-
ars,
And he's got a quarter of a million dollars!
Forrester!
(SPLASH! SPLASH!)

Forrester ducked without thinking, then relaxed. He allowed them to drench him with the warm, scented water. 'Enjoy, enjoy!' he cried, grinning at the bare bodies. Bronze and ivory, lean or soft, every body was beautiful. He knew that none of them would think the worse of him if he touched the two snaps at throat and waist and stepped out of his clothes to join them. But he also knew that his body would not compare well with those of the Adonises, would not impress the full-breasted Venuses, and so he stayed on the rim. 'Drink and be merry, for yesterday we died,' he called and squirted them at random with his joymaker. He didn't mind that he was not as beautiful as they. At least, not at this moment. He was happy. Nothing was troubling him Not worry, not weariness, not fear. Not even his conscience; for, although he was wasting time, he had a right to waste time.

Hara had said so. 'Relax,' advised Hara. 'Get acclimated. Go slow. You've been dead a long time.'

Forrester was well content to follow his advice. In the morning he would take things seriously. In the morning he would go out into this new world and make a place for himself. With unassuming pride he thought that he would do this not because he really needed to, for he had that quarter of a million dollars, all right, but because it was proper that he should work and earn joy. He would be a good citizen.

Experimentally he shouted what he thought of as a friendly obscene suggestion to one of the girls (although Hara had said that the talk of this time contained no obscenities). In return she made a charming gesture, which Forrester tried to think of as an obscene one, and her companion, stretched out at the edge of the pool, drowsily lifted his joymaker and drenched Forrester with a tingling spray that, startlingly, brought him to an instant thrill of sexual excitement and then left him replete and momentarily exhausted.

What a delightful way to live, Forrester thought. He

turned and walked away, followed by more of the shouted
song:

> *And he slept and he slept and he slept,*
> *And he wept and he wept and he wept –*
> *Is he damning? Is he dooming?*
> *For that matter, is he human?*
> *Forrester!*

But he was too far away for them to splash him now and
he had seen someone he wanted to talk to.

It was a girl. She had just come in and was still rather
sober. She was alone. And she was not quite as tall as Forrester himself.

Hara would introduce him to her if asked, Forrester
knew, since this was more or less Hara's party. But he did
not at that moment see Hara. Didn't need Hara, either, he
decided. He walked up to the girl and touched her on the
arm.

'I am Charles D. Forrester,' he said. 'I am five hundred
and ninety-six years old. I have a quarter of a million
dollars. This is my first day out of the sleep-freeze, and I
would appreciate it if you would sit down and talk to me for
a while, or kiss me.'

'Certainly,' she said, taking his hand. 'Let's lie down here
on the violets. Careful of my joymaker; it's loaded with
something special.'

Half an hour later Hara came by and found them, lying
on their backs, each with an arm under the other, heads
inclined toward each other.

Forrester noticed him at once, but went on talking to the
girl. They had been plucking and eating the glass-clear
grapes from a vine over their heads. The intoxicating fruit,
the occasion, and his general sense of well-being combined
to erase social obligations from his mind. Anyway, Hara
would understand and forgive any offense. 'Don't mind him,

11

dear,' Forrester said to the girl. 'You were telling me not to sign up as a donor.'

'Or as game. A lot of greenhorns fall for that, because the money's good. But the way they get you is that you don't figure what it will cost in the long run.'

'That's very interesting,' said Forrester, then sighed, looked away from the girl, and nodded up at Hara. 'You know, Hara,' he said, 'you're a drag.'

'And you're a drunk,' said Hara. 'Hello, Tip. You two seem to be getting on well enough.'

'He's nice,' the girl said. 'Of course, you're nice too, Tip. Is it time for the champagne wine yet?'

'Well past. That's why I came looking for you. I went to a lot of trouble to get this champagne wine for the party, and Forrester will damn well get up and drink some to show the rest of us how it's done.'

'You tilt,' said Forrester, 'and you pour.'

Hara looked at him more carefully, then shook his head and fingered his joymaker. 'Don't you remember anything I tell you?' he chided, spraying Forrester with what felt for a moment like an invigorating, and not at all shocking, ice-cold shower. 'Not too drunk tonight. Get adjusted. Don't forget you were dead. Do what I tell you, will you? And now let's see about this champagne wine.'

Forrester got up like an obedient child and trailed after Hara toward the dispensing tables, one arm around the girl. She had pale hair, up in a fluffy crown, and the tricks of the lighting made it look as though fireflies nested in it.

In the event that he ever saw his once and potentially future wife Dorothy again, Forrester thought, he might have to give this sort of thing up. But for the time being it was very pleasant. And reassuring. It was hard for him to remember, when he had an arm around a pretty girl, that ninety days before his body had been a cryogenic crystal in an ambience of liquid helium, with his heart stopped and his brain still and his lungs a clot of destroyed scar tissue.

He popped the cork of the champagne like a good fellow,

toasted, and drank. He had never seen the label before, but it was champagne, all right. At Hara's request he roared the verses of 'The Bastard King of England', amid much applause, and would not let anyone sober him although he knew he was beginning again to reel and stammer. 'You decadent sods,' he bellowed amiably, 'you know so much! But you don't know how to get drunk.'

They were dancing, a linked circle of all twenty-odd of them, with foot-stamping and sudden changes of direction a little like a morris dance, a little like a Paul Jones, to music like pizzicato cello and the piping of flutes. The girl cried, 'Oh, Charles! Charles Forrester! You almost make an Arcadian of me!' He nodded and grinned, clinging to her on his right and to a huge creature in orange tights on his left, a man who, someone said, had just returned from Mars and was stumbling and straining in Earth's gravity. But he was laughing. Everyone was laughing. A lot of them seemed to be laughing at Forrester, perhaps at his clumsy attempts to follow the step, but no one laughed louder than he.

That was almost the last he remembered. There was some shouting about what to do with him, a proposal to sober him up, a veto, a long giggling debate while he nodded and nodded happily like a pottery head on a spring. He did not know when the party ended. He had a dreamlike memory of the girl leading him across an empty way between tall dark structures like monuments, while he shouted and sang to the echoes. He remembered kissing the girl, and that some vagrant aphrodisiac wisp from her joymaker had filled him with a confused emotion of mingled desire and fear. But he did not remember returning to his room or going to sleep.

And when he awoke in the morning he was buoyant, rested, vigorous, and alone.

TWO

The bed in which Forrester awoke was oval, springy, and gently warm. It woke him by purring faintly at him, soothingly and cheerfully. Then as he began to stir the purring sound stopped, and the surface beneath his body gently began to knead his muscles. Lights came on. There was a distant sound of lively music, like a Gypsy trio. Forrester stretched, yawned, explored his teeth with his tongue, and sat up.

'Good morning, Man Forrester,' said the bed. 'It is eight-fifty hours, and you have an appointment at nine seventy-five. Would you like me to tell you your calls?'

'Not now,' said Forrester at once. Hara had told him about the talking bed. It did not startle him. It was a convenience, not a threat. It was one more comfortable part of this very amiable world.

Forrester, who had been thirty-seven years old when he was burned to death and still considered that to be his age, lit a cigarette, considered his situation carefully, and decided that it was a state unmatched by any other thirty-seven-year-old man in the history of the world. He had it made. Life. Health. Good company. And a quarter of a million dollars.

He was not, of course, as unique as he thought. But as he had not yet fully accepted the fact that he had himself been dead and was now returned to life, much less that there were millions upon millions like him, it *felt* unique. It felt very good.

'I have just received another message for you, Man Forrester,' said the bed.

'Save it,' said Forrester. 'After I have a cup of coffee.'

'Do you wish me to send you a cup of coffee, Man Forrester?'

'You're a nag, you know that? I'll tell you what I want and when I want it.'

What Forrester really wanted, although he had not articulated it even to himself, was to go on enjoying for a moment the sensation of being uncommitted. It was like a liberation. It was like that first week of basic training, in the Army, when he realized that there was a hard way to get through his hitch and an easy one, and that the easy one, which entailed making no decisions of his own and taking no initiative, but merely doing what he was told, was like nothing so much as a rather prolonged holiday in a somewhat poorly equipped summer camp for adults.

Here the accommodations were in fact sumptuous. But the principle was the same. He did not have to concern himself with obligations. He had no obligations. He didn't have to worry about making sure the kids got up for school, because he no longer had any children. He didn't have to think about whether his wife had enough money to get through the day, because he didn't now have a wife. If he wanted to, he could now lie back, pull the covers over his head, and go to sleep. No one would stop him, no one would be aggrieved. If he chose, he could get drunk, attempt the seduction of a girl, or write a poem. All of his debts were paid – or forgiven, centuries since. Every promise was redeemed – or had passed beyond the chance of redemption. The lie he had told Dorothy about that weekend in 1962 need trouble him no longer. If the truth now came out, no one would care; and it was all but impossible that the truth should ever come out.

He had, in short, a blank check on life.

More than that, he had a pretty substantially underwritten guarantee of continuing life itself. He wasn't sick. He wasn't even threatened; even the lump on his leg which he had once or twice gazed on with some worry in the days before his death, could not be malignant or threatening; if it had been, the doctors at the dormer would have fixed it. He need not even worry about being run over by a car – if there were

15

cars – since at worst that might mean only another few centuries in the bath of liquid helium, and then back to life – better than ever!

He had, in fact, everything he had ever wished for.

The only things he didn't have were those he had not wished for because he already had them ... Family. Friends. Position in the community.

In this life of the year A.D. 2527, Charles Forrester was entirely free. But he was not so joyous as to be blinded to the fact that this coin of his treasure had two sides. Another way of looking at it was that he was entirely superfluous.

'Man Forrester,' said the bed, 'I must insist. I have both an urgent-class message and a personal-visit notice.' And the mattress curled under him, humped itself, and deposited him on the floor of the room.

Staggering, Forrester growled, 'What's urgent?'

'A hunting license has been taken out on you, Man Forrester. The licensee is Heinzlichen Jura de Syrtis Major, male, dipara-Zen, Utopian, eighty-six elapsed, six feet four inches, import-export. He is extraterrestrial-human. No reason declared. Bonds and guaranties have been posted. Would you like your coffee now?'

While the bed was speaking it had been rolling itself into the wall. It disappeared into a sphincter that closed and left no trace. This was disconcerting, but Forrester remembered Hara's instructions, searched for and found his joymaker, and said to it, 'I would like my breakfast now. Ham and eggs. Toast and orange juice. Coffee. And a pack of cigarettes.'

'They will be delivered in five minutes, Man Forrester,' said the joymaker. 'May I give you the rest of your messages?'

'Wait a minute. I thought it was the bed that was giving me messages.'

'We are all the same, Man Forrester. Your messages follow. Notice of personal visit: Taiko Hironibi will join

16

you for breakfast. Dr Hara has prescribed a euphoric in case of need, which will be delivered with your breakfast. Adne Bensen sends you a kiss. First Merchants Audi and Trust invites your patronage. Society of Ancients states you have been approved for membership and relocation benefits. Ziegler Durant and Colfax Attornies—'

'You can skip the commercials. What was that about a hunting license?'

'A hunting license has been taken out on you, Man Forrester. The licensee is Heinzlichen Jura de—'

'You said that. Wait a minute.' Forrester regarded his joymaker thoughtfully. The principle of it was clear enough. It was a remote input-output station for a shared-time computer program, with certain attachments that functioned as pocket flask, first-aid kit, cosmetic bag, and so on. It looked something like a mace or a jester's scepter. Forrester told himself that it was really no less natural to talk to something like a mace than it was to talk into something like a telephone. But at the other end of a telephone had been a human being . . . or at least, he reminded himself, the taped voice of what at one time had been a human being . . . Anyway, it didn't *feel* natural. He said guardedly, 'I don't understand all this. I don't know who these people are who are calling me up, either.'

'Man Forrester, the personal callers are as follows. Taiko Hironibi: male, dendritic Confucian, Arcadian, fifty-one elapsed, six feet one inch, organizer, business political. He will bring his own breakfast. Adne Bensen: female, Universalist Arcadian-Trimmer, twenty-three declared, five feet seven inches, experiencer-homeswoman, no business stated. Her kiss follows.'

Forrester did not know what to expect but was pleasantly ready for anything.

What he got was indeed a kiss. It was disconcerting. No kissing lips were visible. There was a hint of perfumed breath, then a pressure on his lips – warm and soft, moist and sweet.

17

Startled, he touched his mouth. 'How the devil did you do that?' he shouted.

'Sensory stimulation through the tactile net, Man Forrester. Will you receive Taiko Hironibi?'

'Well,' said Forrester, 'frankly, I don't know. Oh, hell. I guess so. Send him in . . . Wait a minute. Shouldn't I get dressed first?'

'Do you wish other clothing, Man Forrester?'

'Don't confuse me. Just hold on a minute,' he said, rattled and angry. He thought for a minute. 'I don't know who this Hirowatsis is—'

'Taiko Hironibi, Man Forrester. Male, dendritic Confucian—'

'Cut that out!' Forrester was breathing hard. Abruptly the joymaker in his hand hissed and sprayed him with something that felt damp for a second, then dissipated.

Forrester felt himself relaxing. He appreciated the tranquilizing spray, without quite liking the idea of having a machine prescribe and dispense it.

'Oh, *God*,' he said, 'what do I care who he is? Go ahead. Send him in. And get a move on with my breakfast, will you?'

'You'll do!' cried Taiko Hironibi. 'The greatest! What a cranial index! You look – cripes, I don't know what to call it – you look like a brain. But a swinger.'

Charles Forrester, gravely and cheerfully, indicated a seat with his hand. 'Sit down. I don't know what you want but I'm willing to talk about it. You're the damnedest looking Japanese I ever saw.'

'Really?' The man looked disconcerted. He also looked quite non-Japanese: crew-cut golden hair, blue eyes. 'They change you around so,' he said apologetically. 'Maybe I used to look different. Say! Did I get here first?'

'You got here before my breakfast, even.'

'Great! That's really great. Now, here's the thing. We're all messed up here, you have to get that straight right away.

18

The people are sheep. They know they're being ex-propriated, but do they do anything about it? Sweat, no, they sit back and enjoy it. That's what we're for in the Ned Lud Society. I don't know your politics, Charley—'

'I used to be a Democrat, mostly.'

'—Well, you can forget that. It doesn't matter. I'm regis-tered Arcadian myself, of course, but a lot of the guys are Trimmers, maybe—' he winked – 'maybe even something a little worse, you know? We're all in this together. Affects everybody. If you raise your kids with machines you're bound to have machine-lovers growing up, right? Now—'

'Hcy!' said Forrester, looking at his wall. At a point as near as he could remember to be just about where the bed had disappeared, a sphincter was opening again. It dis-gorged a table set for two, one side bearing his breakfast, the other a complete setting but no food.

'Ah, breakfast,' said Taiko Hironibi. He opened a pouch in the kiltlike affair he wore and took out a small capped bowl, a plastic box that turned out to contain something like crackers, and a globe, which, when squeezed, poured a hot, watery, greenish tea into the cup at his place. 'Care for a pickled plum?' he asked politely, removing the cap from the bowl.

Forrester shook his head. Chairs had appeared beside the table, and he slid into the one placed before the ham and eggs.

Next to the steaming plate was a small crystal tray con-taining a capsule and a scrap of golden paper on which was written:

I don't know much about that champagne wine. Take this if you have a hungover.

Hara

To the best of Forrester's knowledge he didn't have a hangover, but the capsule looked too good to waste. He swallowed it with some of the orange juice and at once felt

19

even more relaxed. If that were possible. He felt positively affectionate toward the blond Japanese, now decorously nibbling at a dark, withered object.

It crossed Forrester's mind that the capsule, plus what the joymaker had sprayed him with, might add up to something larger that he was ready for. He felt almost giddy. Better guard against that, he thought, and demanded as unpleasantly as he could, 'Who sent you here?'

'Why – the contact was Adne Bensen.'

'Don't know her,' snapped Forrester trying not to grin.

'You don't?' Taiko stopped eating, dismayed. 'Sweat, man, she told me you'd be—'

'Doesn't matter,' cried Forrester, and prepared for the killing question he had been saving. 'Just tell me this. What's the advantage of my joining your society?'

The blond man was clearly disgruntled. 'Listen, I'm not *begging* you. We got something good here. You want in, come in. You want out, go—'

'No don't give me an argument. Just answer the question.' Forrester managed to light a cigarette, puffed smoke in Taiko's face. 'For instance,' he said, 'would it be money that's involved?'

'Well, sure. Everybody needs money, right? But that's not the only thing—'

Forrester said, politely but severely, restraining the impulse to giggle, 'You know, I had an idea it would be like that.' His two tranquilizers, plus what was still in his system from the previous night, were adding up to something very close to a roaring drunk, he noticed. With some pride. How manly of him, he thought, to keep his wits so clear when he was so smashed.

'You act like I'm trying to take advantage of you,' Taiko said angrily. 'What's the matter with you? Don't you see that the machines are depriving us of our natural human birthright? to be miserable if we want to, to make mistakes, to forget things? Don't you see that we Luddites want to smash the machines and give the world back to *people*? I

20

mean, not counting the *necessary* machines, of course.'

'Sure I see,' agreed Forrester, standing up and swaying slightly. 'Well, thanks. You better be going now, Hironibi. I'll think over what you said, and maybe we can get together some time. But don't you call me. Let me call you.' And he bowed Taiko to the door and watched it close behind him, keeping his face relaxed until the Japanese was gone.

Then Forrester bent over and howled with laughter. 'Con man!' he shouted. 'He thinks I'm an easy mark! Ah, the troubles of the rich – always somebody trying to swindle you out of it!'

'I do not understand, Man Forrester,' said the joymaker. 'Are you addressing me?'

'Not in this life,' Forrester told the machine, still chuckling. He was filled with a growing pride. He might look like a country cousin, he thought, but there went one sharper who had got no farther than first base.

He wondered who this Adne Bensen was who had fingered him for the swindler and sent him an electronic kiss. If she kissed in person the way she kissed through sensory stimulation of the tactile net, she might be worth knowing. And no problem, either. If Taiko was the worst this century could turn up, Forrester thought with pleasure and joy, his quarter of a million dollars was safe!

Twenty minutes later he found his way to the street level of the building, not without arguments from his joymaker. 'Man Forrester,' it said, sounding almost aggrieved, 'it is better to take a taxi! Do not walk. The guaranties do not apply to provocation and contributory negligence.'

'Shut up for a minute, will you?' Forrester managed to get the door open and looked out.

The city of A.D. 2527 was very large, very fast-moving, and very noisy. Forrester was standing in a sort of driveway. A clump of ethereal thirty-foot-high ferns in front of him partially masked a twelve-lane highway packed to its margins with high-speed traffic moving in both directions.

21

Occasionally a vehicle would cut in to the entrance to his building, pause before him for a moment, and then move on. Taxis? Forrester wondered. If so, he was giving them no encouragement.

'Man Forrester,' said the joymaker, 'I have summoned death-reversal equipment, but it will not arrive for several minutes. I must warn you, the costs may be challenged under the bonding regulations.'

'Oh, shut up.' It seemed to be a warm day, and Forrester was perhaps still slightly befuddled; the temptation to walk was irresistible. All questions could be deferred. Should be deferred, he told himself. Obviously his first task was to get himself oriented. And – he prided himself on this – he had been something of a cosmopolitan, back in those days before his death, equally at home in San Francisco or Rome as in New York or Chicago. And he had always made time to stroll around a city.

He would stroll through this one now. Joymakers be damned, thought Charles Forrester; he right-faced, hooked the joymaker to his belt, and set off along a narrow pedestrian walk.

There were very few walkers. It didn't do to make snap judgments, Forrester thought, but these people seemed soft. Perhaps they could afford to be. No doubt someone like himself, he mused soberly, seemed like a hairy troglodyte, crude, savage, flint-axed.

'Man Forrester!' cried the joymaker from his belt. 'I must inform you that Heinzlichen Jura de Syrtis Major has waived protest of the bonding regulations. The death-reversal equipment is on its way.' He slapped it, and it was quiet, or else its continued bleating was drowned out by the sound of the clamouring traffic. Whatever drove these cars, it was not gasoline. There were no fumes. There was only a roar of air and singing tires, multiplied a hundredfold and unending. The trafficway lay between tall bright buildings, one a soft, glowing orange, one the crystalline, blue-gray color of fractured steel. In the court of a building across the

22

trafficway he could see, dimly through the glass and the momentary gaps in the traffic, a riot of plant growth with enormous scarlet fruits. On a balcony above him scented fountains played.

The joymaker was addressing him again, but he could catch only part of it. '. . . In station now, Man Forrester.' A shadow passed over him, and he looked up.

Overhead a white aircraft of some sort – it had no wings – was sliding diagonally down toward him. It bore a glittering ruby insigne like the serpent staff of Aesculapius on its side. The nearer end of it was all glass and exposed, and inside a young woman in crisply tailored blue was drowsily watching something on a screen invisible to Forrester. She looked up, gazed at him, spoke into a microphone, then glanced at him again, and went back to watching her screen. The vehicle took position over his head and waited, following with him as he walked.

'That's funny,' said Forrester aloud.

'It's a funny world,' said somebody quite near him.

He turned around. Four men were standing there, looking at him with pleasant, open expressions. One of them was very tall and very heavy. In fact, he was gross. He leaned on a cane, studying Forrester, his expression alert and interested.

Forrester realized that he was the one who had spoken and, in the same moment, realized that he knew him. 'Oh sure,' he said. 'The Martian in orange tights.'

'Very good,' said the Martian, nodding. He was not in orange tights now; he wore a loose white tunic and slate-gray shorts. He wasn't really a Martian, Forrester remembered; at least, his ancestors had come from Earth.

One of the other men took Forrester's hand and shook it. 'You're the one with the quarter of a million dollars,' he said. 'Look me up when this is all over. I'd like to know what a fellow like you thinks of our world.'

He brought his knee up and kicked Forrester in the groin. Hard.

Forrester felt the world explode, starting inside him. He saw that the man was stepping back, looking at him with interest and pleasure; but it was hard to watch him because the city was moving. It tilted up at an angle, and the sidewalk struck him on the forehead. He rolled, clutching at his testicles, and found himself looking upward.

The man from Mars said conversationally, 'Don't hurry. Plenty of time for everybody.' He lifted his cane and limped forward. Moving was quite an effort for him in Earth's gravity, after Mars, Forrester saw. The cane came down on his shoulder and upper arm, was lifted and came down again, regularly, slowly, and strongly. It must have been weighted. It felt like a baseball bat.

The pain in Forrester's gut was like death. His arm was numb.

All in all, though, he realized quite clearly – unable to move, watching as they passed the cane from hand to hand and the white aircraft hovered overhead, the woman's face peering patiently down – all in all, it was hurting rather less than he might have expected. Perhaps it was Hara's hungover medicine. Perhaps it was just shock.

'You were warned, Man Forrester,' said the joymaker sadly from where it lay beside his head.

He tried to speak, but his lungs were not working.

He could not quite lose consciousness, either, though he wanted to very much. Perhaps that was another result of Hara's euphoric pill. Then he felt that he was succeeding. The pain in his belly grew alarmingly and began to recede again, and then he felt nothing at all, or nothing physical.

But there was something painful in his mind, something that whimpered, *Why? Why me?*

THREE

Howls of laughter rolled over Forrester. A girl was screaming, 'He's spinning it! He's spinning it! Gee, I think I saw the cartridge!'

Forrester opened his eyes. He was in something that lurched and hummed. A girl in a tailored blue suit, her back to him, was staring at what seemed to be a television screen showing a sort of arena, where the screaming girl, face flushed and happy, stamping with excitement, was standing over a blindfolded man who held a gun.

Forrester's aches and bruises reminded him at once of what had happened. He was surprised that he was still alive. He croaked, 'Hey!'

The girl in tailored blue looked over her shoulder at him. 'You're all right,' she said. 'Just take it easy. We'll be there in a minute.'

'Where?'

Impatiently she moved her hand. The arena with the man and girl disappeared – just as the man seemed to be raising the gun – and Forrester found himself looking at blue sky and clouds. 'Lift up a little,' the girl in blue said. 'You'll see it. There.'

Forrester tried to raise himself on an elbow, caught a glimpse of trees and rambling pastel buildings, and fell back. 'I can't lift myself up! Damn it, I've been half killed.' He became aware that he was on a sort of stretcher and that there was another one beside him. The other one was also occupied, by someone with a sheet over him. 'Who's that?' he cried.

'How would I know? I just bring them in, I don't write their life stories. Now relax, or I'll have to put you to sleep.'

'You silly bitch,' said Forrester precisely. 'I'm not going

to stand for this. I demand that you— Wait a minute! What are you doing?'

The girl had turned around, and she was holding something very like his own joymaker, pointed at him. 'Are you going to shut up and lie still?'

'I warn you! Don't you dare—'

She sighed, and something cool touched his face.

Forrester gathered all his strength to tell her what he thought of her, her probable sex life, and this world of hers, in which arbitrary and unpleasant things were done to well-to-do men like himself. He couldn't. All that came out was, 'Arr, a-r-r-r.' He was not unconscious, but he was very weak.

The girl said, 'You sweat me, greenie. You are a greenhorn, aren't you? I can always tell. You people wake up in the dormer and you think you're God's own sweat. Mother! Sure you're alive. Sure you've had the biggest break you can imagine. But do you think *we* care?'

All this time the aircraft was slipping and turning, coming in for a landing. The girl, who one would have thought to be the pilot, paid no attention. She was very cross. She said, 'Now, I know my job, and my job is to keep you alive – or keep you safely till they can take care of you. I don't have to talk to you. I especially don't have to listen to you.'

Forrester said, 'A-r-r-r.'

'I don't even like you,' she said with vexation, 'and you've made me miss my favorite program. Oh, go to sleep.'

And, just as Forrester felt the aircraft touch ground, she raised the joymaker again, and he did.

At the temperature of liquid helium, chemistry stops.

On this fact, and on one reasonable hope, the largest industry of the late twentieth century had been built.

The reasonable hope was that the progress of medicine in past years would be matched by similar progress in the future – so that, no matter what a person might die of, at some future time a way would be found to cure it, to repair it, or at least to make it irrelevant to continuing life and activity (including a method of repairing the damage done by freezing a body to that temperature).

The fact was that freezing stopped time.

And the industry was Immortality, Inc.

In the city of Shoggo in which Forrester had awakened, a city that was nearly eight hundred years old and enormous, a thousand acres of park along a lake front had humped themselves into a hill. All around was flat. The hill itself was an artifact. It was, as a matter of fact, the freezing center for that part of the world.

A hundred and fifty million cubic yards of earth had been eaten out of the ground to make a cold-storage locker for people. After the locker was built, most of the dirt was heaped back on top of it for insulation.

The differential in temperature between ground level and the heart of the frozen hill was nearly five hundred degrees, Fahrenheit, or three hundred and more in the Kelvin scale on which the dormer operated.

When Forrester realized where the white aircraft had taken him, he was instantly submerged in a terror he could not express. Beginning to awaken, he was still terribly weak, as though one of those sprays from the girl's joymaker had shorted out ninety percent of his volitional muscle control. (As in fact it had.) When he saw the bright featureless ceiling overhead and heard the moan and click of the thousand frightening instruments that brought people back to life, he fugued into a terrifying certainty that they were going to freeze him again. He lay there, groaning inarticulately, while things were done to him.

But they were not freezing him.

They were just patching him up. The blood was washed away. The bruises were scrubbed with something metallic, then touched with a transparent stiff jelly from a long silvery tube that looked something like a large lipstick. His left thigh was pressed for a moment between two glowing screens, which he knew to be a sort of X-ray device, and a fine wash of something that glistened wet and dark was painted over his heart.

This last treatment made him feel better, whatever it was. He found that he was able to speak.

'Thank you,' he said.

The young-looking, red-faced man who was working over him at that moment nodded casually and touched Forrester's navel with the end of a silvery probe. He glanced at it and said, 'All right, I guess we're through with you. Get up, and let's see if you can walk to Hara's office.'

Forrester swung his legs out of the sort of low-walled crib he was lying in and found he could walk as well as ever. Even his bruises didn't hurt, or not much, although he could detect what seemed to be the beginning return of pain.

The red-faced man said, 'You're fine. Stay out of here for a while, will you? And don't forget to see Hara, because you're in some kind of trouble.' He turned away as Forrester started to question him. 'How would I know what kind? Just go see Hara.'

Although a slim green arrowhead of light skipped along the floor ahead of him, guiding him to Hara's office, Forrester thought he could have found it without the arrowhead. Once he left the emergency rooms he was in the part of the dormer he remembered. Here he had wakened out of a frozen sleep lasting half a millennium. There, every day for a week, he had gone bathing in some sort of light, warm oil that had vibrated and tingled, making him feel drowsy but stronger each day. It was on the level below this that he had done his exercises and in the building across the bed of poinsettias (except that these poinsettias were bright gold) that he had slept.

He wondered what had become of the rest of what he thought of as his graduating class. The thawed Lazaruses were processed in batches – fifty at a clip in his group – and, although he had not spent much time with any of them, there was something about this shared experience that had made him know them quickly.

28

But when they were discharged, they all went in separate directions, apparently for policy reasons. Forrester regretted they had lost touch.

Then he laughed out loud. A blue-jacketed woman, walking toward him along the hall and talking into an instrument on her wrist, looked up at him with curiosity and faint contempt. 'Sorry,' he said to her still chuckling, as the green beacon of light turned a corner and he followed. He didn't doubt he looked peculiar. He felt peculiar. He was amused that he was missing these fellow graduates of the freezatorium with the fond, distant detachment he had felt for his high school class. Yet it was less than forty-eight hours since he had been with them.

A busy forty-eight hours, he thought. A bit frightening, too. Even wealth was not as secure a buffer against this world as he had thought.

The flickering green light led him into Hara's office and disappeared.

Hara was standing at the door, waiting for him. 'Damned kamikaze,' he said amiably. 'Can't I trust you out of my sight for a minute?'

Forrester, who had never been a demonstrative man, seized his hand and shook it. 'Jesus, I'm glad to see you! I'm mixed up. I don't know what the hell is going on, and—'

'Just stay out of trouble, will you? Sit down.' Hara made a seat come out of the wall and a bottle out of his desk. He thumbed the cork expertly and poured a drink for Forrester, saying, 'I expected you under your own power this morning, you know. Not in a DR cart. Didn't the center warn you somebody was after you?'

'Positively not!' Forrester was both startled and indignant. 'What do you mean, somebody was after me? I had no idea—'

Then, tardily, recognition dawned. 'Unless,' he finished thoughtfully, 'that's what the joymaker was mumbling about. It was all about bonds and guaranties and somebody

29

named Heinz something of Syrtis Major. That's on Mars, isn't it? *Say!*'

'Heinzlichen Jura de Syrtis Major,' Hara supplied, toasting Forrester with his glass and taking a tiny sip of the drink. Forrester followed suit; it was champagne again. Hara sighed and said, 'I don't know, Charles, but I don't think I'll acquire a taste for this stuff after all.'

'Never mind that! The Martian! The fellow in orange tights! He's the one who beat me up, he and his gang!'

Hara looked faintly puzzled. 'Why, of course.'

Forrester tipped up his ruby crystal glass and drained the champagne. It was not very good champagne – heaven knew where Hara had found it, after Forrester had mentioned it as being one of the great goods of the past – and it was by no means appropriate to the occasion. It tickled his nose. But at least it contained alcohol, which Forrester felt he needed.

He said, humbly, 'Please explain what happened.'

'Sweat, Charles, where do I start? What did you do to Heinzie?'

'Nothing! I mean–well, nothing, really. I might have stepped on his feet when we were dancing.'

Hara said angrily, 'A *Marsman*? You stepped on his *feet*?'

'What's so bad about that? I mean, even if I did. I'm not sure I did. Would you blow your stack about something like that?'

'Mars isn't Shoggo,' Hara said patiently, 'and, anyway, maybe I would. Depends. Did you read your orientation book?'

'Huh?'

'The book of information about the year 2527. You got it when you were discharged here.'

Forrester searched his memory. 'Oh, that. Maybe I left it at the party.'

'Well, that adds,' Hara said with some disgust. 'Will you please try to bear in mind, first, that you're sort of my responsibility; second, that you don't know your way around?

I'll see you get another copy of the book. Read it! Come back and see me tomorrow; I've got work to do now. On your way out, stop at the discharge office and pick up your stuff.'

He escorted Forrester to the door, turned, then paused.

'Oh. Adne Bensen sends regards. Nice girl. She likes you,' he said, closed the door, and was gone.

Forrester completed his processing and was released by the medical section, receiving as he left a neat white folder with his name imprinted in gold.

It contained four sets of documents. One was a sheaf of medical records; the second was the book Hara had mentioned, slim and bronze-bound, with the title printed in luminous letters:

YOUR GUIDE TO THE 26TH CENTURY
[1970–1990 EDITION]

The third document seemed to be a legal paper of some kind. At least, it was backed with a sheet of stiff blue material that gave it the look of a subpoena. Forrester remembered that the doctor who had patched him up had spoken of trouble. This looked like the trouble, though the words were either unfamiliar in context or totally meaningless to him:

You, Charles Dalgleish Forrester, uncommitted, undeclared, elapsed thirty-seven years, unemployed-pending, take greeting and are directed. Requirement: To be present at Congruency Hearing, hours 1075, days 15, months 9 ...

It had the authentic feel of legalese, he saw with dismay. Much of the face of the single sheet of paper that the blue material enclosed was covered with a sort of angular, almost readable lettering – something like the machine script they

31

used to put on checks, Forrester thought, and then realized that that was no doubt what it was.

But the paper had a date on it, and since that date appeared to be a week or more away, as near as Forrester could figure, he tabled it with some relief and turned to the next and last item in the folder.

This was a financial statement. Attached to it was a crisp metallic slip with the same angular printing on it, which Forrester recognized as a check.

He fingered it lovingly and puzzled out the amount.

It was made out to him, and it was for $231,057.56.

Forrester attempted to fold it – it sprang back like spring steel – and then put it away flat in his pocket. It felt good there.

He was faintly puzzled by the fact that it was some twenty thousand dollars less than he had expected. But in terms of percentage the amount didn't seem very significant, and he was cheerfully reconciled to the opinion that this society, like all societies, would no doubt have some sort of taxes. Twenty grand was, after all, an amount he could well afford as a sort of initiation fee.

Feeling much more secure, he emerged into the sunlight and looked about him.

It was late afternoon. The sun was to his right. Slate-blue water stretched to his left. He was looking southward over the great pinnacled mass of the city.

Aircraft moved above it. Things crawled in its valleys. The sun picked out reflections from glass and metal, and, although it was still daylight, the city already exuded a developing glow of neon and fluorescence.

There were at least ten million people in Shoggo, Forrester knew. There were theaters and card parties and homes, places where he might find a friend or a lover. Or even an enemy. Down there was the girl who had kissed him last night – Tip? – and the crazy Martian and his gang, who had tried to kill him.

But where?

Forrester did not know where to begin.

Alive, healthy, with almost a quarter of a million dollars in his pocket, he felt left out of things. Standing on a planet with a population of seventeen billion active human beings, and at least twice that number dreaming in the slow cold of the helium baths, he felt entirely alone.

From his belt the voice of the joymaker spoke up. 'Man Forrester. Will you take your messages?'

'Yes,' said Forrester, disconcerted. 'No. Wait a minute.'

He took the last cigarette out of the pack he had got that morning, lit it, then crumpled the pack and threw it away. He thought.

Owning a joymaker was a little like having a genie with three wishes. The thing's promptness and precision disconcerted him; he felt that it demanded equal certitude from himself and he did not feel up to it.

He grinned to himself ruefully, admitting that he was being made self-conscious by what he really knew to be nothing but a radio connection with some distant lash-up of cold-state transistors and ferrite cores. Finally he said, 'Look. You. I think what I ought to do is go back to my room and start over again from home base. What's the best way to get there?'

'Man Forrester,' said the joymaker, 'the best way to get to the room you occupied is by cab, which I can summon for you. However, the room is no longer yours. Will you accept your messages?'

'No. Wait a minute! What do you mean, no longer mine? I didn't check out.'

'Not necessary, Man Forrester. It is automatic on departure.'

He paused and thought, and on consideration it didn't seem to matter much. He had left nothing there. No bag, no baggage. No personal possessions, not even a shaving brush: he wouldn't have to shave for a week or two anyway, Hara had told him.

All of himself that he had left in the room was the

garments he had worn last night. And those, he remembered, were disposable ... and so had no doubt been disposed of.

'What about the bill?' he asked.

'The charge was paid by the West Annex Discharge Center. It is entered on your financial statement, Man Forrester. Your messages include one urgent, two personal, one notice of legal, seven commercial—'

'I don't want to hear right now. Wait a minute.'

Once again Forrester tried to frame the right question.

He abandoned the effort. Whatever his skills, he was not a computer programmer, and it was no good trying to talk like one. It seemed absurd to ask a machine for value judgments, but—

'Cripes,' he said, 'tell me something. What would you do, *right now*, if you were me?'

The joymaker answered without hesitation, as though that sort of question were coming up every day. 'If I were you, Man Forrester, which is to say, if I were human, just unfrozen, without accommodations, lacking major social contacts, unemployed, unskilled—'

'That's the picture, all right,' Forrester agreed. 'So answer the question.' Something was crawling underfoot. He stepped aside, out of its way, a glittering metal thing.

'I would go to a tea shop, Man Forrester. I would then read my orientation book while enjoying a light meal. I would then think things over. I would then—'

'That's far enough.'

The metal thing, apparently espying Forrester's discarded cigarette pack, scuttled over to it and gobbled it down. Forrester watched it for a second, then nodded.

'You've got some good ideas, machine,' he said. 'Take me to a tea shop!'

FOUR

The joymaker procured a cab for Forrester, a wingless vehicle like the death-reversal conveyance that had brought him in for repair, but orange and black instead of white; it looked like Hallowe'en. And the cab took him to the joymaker's recommended tea shop.

The shop was curious. It was located in an interior hall of a great spidery building in the heart of the city. The cab flew under a pierced-steel buttress, actually into a sort of vaulted opening that could have served only birds and angels, or men in aircraft, since it was at least fifty feet above ground. It halted and hovered before a balcony planted with climbing roses, and Forrester had to step over a knife edge of empty space. The cab did not quiver, not even when his weight left it.

A girl with hair like transparent cellophane greeted him. 'I have your reservation, Man Forrester. Will you follow me, please?'

He did, walking behind her across a quartz-pebbled court and into the hall that was the tea room, admiring the swing of her hips and wondering just what it was that she did to her hair to make it stand out like a sculptured puffball and rob it of opacity.

She seated him beside a reflecting pool, with silvery fish swimming slowly about. Even with the peculiar hairdo, she was a pretty girl. She had dimples and dark, amused eyes.

He said, 'I don't know what I want, actually. Anyway, who do I order from?'

'We are all the same, Man Forrester,' she said. 'May I choose for you? Some tea and cakes?'

Numbly, he nodded and, as she turned and left, watched

the sway of her hips with an entirely different kind of interest.

He sighed. This was a confusing world!

He took the book out of the folder he had been given at the West Annex Discharge Center and placed it on the table. Its cover was simple and direct:

YOUR GUIDE TO THE 26TH CENTURY
(1970–1990 EDITION)
Where to Go
How to Live
Managing Your Money
Laws, Customs, Folkways

It was edge-indexed with helpful headings: MAKING FRIENDS, LIVING ON A BUDGET, HOW TO GET THE MOST OUT OF YOUR JOYMAKER, JOB OPPORTUNITIES, WHERE TO GET NEEDED TRAINING . . . it went on and on. Forrester, flipping through the pages, was astonished to find how many of them there were.

He had a good week's reading here, he estimated. Obviously the first thing for him to do was to decide what was the first thing to do.

Making friends could wait a bit. He seemed already to have made more friends – and enemies! – than he could assimilate.

Living on a budget? He smiled to himself and patted the pocket that held his check.

How to get the most out of your joymaker, though. That was a good place to start, thought Forrester, then opened the book to the right page and began to read.

The remote-access computer transponder called the 'joymaker' is your most valuable single possession in your new life. If you can imagine a combination of telephone, credit card, alarm clock, pocket bar, reference library, and full-time secretary, you will have sketched some of the functions provided by your joymaker.

Essentially it is a transponder connecting you with the central computing facilities of the city in which you reside on a shared-time, self-programming basis. 'Shared-time' means that many other joymakers use the same central computer – in Shoggo, something like ten million of them. If you go to another city your joymaker will continue to serve you, but it must be reset to a new frequency and pulse-code. This will be done automatically when you travel by public transportation. However, if you use private means, or if for any reason you spend any time in the agricultural areas, you must notify the joymaker of your intentions. It will inform you of any steps you must take.

'Self-programming' means that the programmed software includes . . .

The self-programming, shared-time girl with the dark, grave eyes brought Forrester his tea and cakes. 'Thank you,' he said, staring at her. He was still not quite sure of his deductions about her. He tried an experiment. 'Can you give me my messages?' he asked.

'Certainly, Man Forrester, if you wish,' she said promptly. 'Alfred Guysman wishes to see you on political business. Adne Bensen asks you to return her message of this morning. The Nineteenth Chromatic Trust informs you that arrangements have been made for you to establish banking facilities with them—'

'That's enough,' he said, marveling at how nicely a shared-time transponder could be packaged. 'I'll take the rest later.'

There was no sugar for the tea, but it was physically hot and chemically cool at the same time – rather like a mentholated cigarette, except that there was no particular taste associated with it. Forrester returned to his book.

'Self-programming' means that the programmed software includes procedures for translating most normal variations of voice, idiom, accent, and other variable modalities into a computer-oriented simscript and thence into the mathematical expressions on which the computers operate. As long as your personal joymaker is within reception range of your voice, you may communicate via other shared-time transponders if you wish. Appropriate modulation will be established automatically. However, do not attempt to use another individual's joymaker when yours is not within range. Proper coding cannot be assured. In the event that your joymaker is lost or damaged . . .

Forrester sighed and ate one of the cakes. It was rich with flavors like butter and cinnamon and with others he could not identify. Pleasant but strange.

Very much like this world that had been given him.

'Man Forrester,' said the joymaker at his belt, its tones muffled by his coat and the tablecloth, 'it is necessary for you to accept some messages. I have a notice of personal visit and—'

Forrester said, 'Look, I'm doing what you said, right? I'm reading my book. Let me figure it out a little before you throw messages at me. Unless,' he said as an afterthought, 'there's some matter of life or death.'

'There are no messages involving life or death, Man Forrester.'

'Then wait awhile.' He was aware – he didn't know how long it had been going on – that a distant wind instrument was hooting faintly. Pleasant but strange. Spiced cool breezes blew from the paneled walls, also pleasant but strange.

He said hesitantly, 'Joymaker, answer me a question. Why did what's-his-name, Heinzie, beat me up?'

'I cannot identify the individual, Man Forrester. You were beaten up by four persons in the one recorded incident of attack. Their names were Shlomo Cassavetes, Heinzlichen Jura de Syrtis Major, Edwardino—'

'That one. Heinzlichen Jura de Syrtis Major. Or, for that matter, all of them – why did they rumble me?'

'I have a priority message regarding Heinzlichen Jura de Syrtis Major, Man Forrester. Perhaps it will be informative. May I give it to you?'

'Oh, hell. Why not?'

'Heinzlichen Jura de Syrtis Major is protesting enforcement of guaranties and has enjoined disbursements under his bond. You are notified, Man Forrester.'

Forrester said hotly, 'That's what you call informative? Look, skip the damned messages and answer the question. What was that scene all about?'

'You have asked three questions, Man Forrester. May I offer a synoptic reply?'

'Please do, old friend.'

'Heinzlichen Jura de Syrtis Major, a guest in the reprooms utilized by Alin Hara, conceived a grievance against you, cause unstated. He called into association Shlomo Cassavetes, Edwardino Wry, and Edwardeto Wry; they formed an ad hoc club and filed appropriate conformance in regard to bonds and guaranties. The intention was stated as murder, first phase, ad lib. The motivation was stated as grievance as to De Syrtis Major, practical joke as to the others. Conformances were recorded, and the subject – that is, yourself, Man Forrester – was notified. Does that answer your three questions, Man Forrester?'

'What do you think?' Forrester snapped. 'Well, maybe it does. Sort of. You mean those other three finks lumped me for a *joke*?'

'They so stated, yes, Man Forrester.'

'And they're still running around loose?'

'Do you wish me to ascertain their present whereabouts, Man Forrester?'

'No – I mean, aren't they in jail or something?'

'No, Man Forrester.'

Forrester said, 'Joymaker, leave me alone for awhile. I better get back to my orientation book. I see I don't know as much as I thought I did.'

Forrester drank the rest of his tea, ate the rest of his cakes, and plowed back into his book.

To use your joymaker as telephone: You must know the ortho-name and identification spectrum of the person you wish to reach. Once you have given this information to the joymaker it will be remembered, and you can then refer to the person in later calls by a reciprocal name or any other personal identification programmed into your joymaker. If you have been called by any person, the joymaker will have recorded the necessary ortho-name and identification spectrum. Simply ask the joymaker to call the person you wish to speak to. If you wish to establish a priority rating with any person, that person must so inform his joymaker. Otherwise your calls may be deferred or canceled as directed by the called person.

To use your joymaker as credit card: You must know the institutional designation and account spectrum . . .

A belated thought percolated to the surface of Forrester's mind. Messages. Financial institutions. One of the messages had been from something that sounded like that.

He sighed and looked around the room. Most of the tables were empty. But it was a large room, and there were perhaps fifty other people in it, all of them seated at tables in twos and threes and larger groups. Through some effect of the sound-conditioning, he could not hear their voices, only the distant hooting flute and a faint splashing from the giant fish in the reflecting pools.

He wondered if any of these fifty people would mind if he got up and walked over to them.

Touching the faintly sore spots on his shoulders and neck, he decided against trying it. But it gave him an idea, and he turned to the section of the book called MAKING FRIENDS.

'I have an *urgent* notice of personal visit, Man Forrester,' grumbled the joymaker from his waist.

'Just save it,' said Forrester, preoccupied. He was startled at the length of the list of ways of making friends. Above all, there were clubs. Clubs in such profusion that he wondered that even seventeen billion people could fill their rolls. Social clubs, gymnastic clubs, professional clubs. Political groups, religious groups, therapeutic groups. There was a Society of First Families of Mars, and a Loyal Order of Descendants of Barsoom Fans. There were forty-eight bird-watching groups in Shoggo alone. There were stamp collectors and coin collectors and tax-token collectors and jet-car-transfer collectors.

There was something called the Society of Ancients that looked interesting, as it appeared to be an organization of persons like Forrester himself, revived from the dead heart of the freezers. Yet it was listed along with such curiosities as the B.P.O.E. and the Industrial Workers of the World (Memorial Association) in small type at the end of the section.

Puzzling. If it existed at all, should it not have a membership in the billions?

Evidently it did not, but . . .

'Man Forrester,' shrilled the joymaker, 'I must inform you of personal visitation by—'

'Wait a minute,' said Forrester, suddenly looking up, startled.

There was a hint of perfume in the air.

Forrester put down his book, frowning. The scent was familiar. What was it? Another tactile-tape message from this Adne Bensen, whoever she might be?

He felt a touch on his shoulder, then warm arms around him, a hug.

These tactile tapes were certainly convincing, he thought momentarily, then realized this was not a tape. He was not merely feeling and smelling the presence of the embracing arms. He saw them, from the corner of his eye and,

41

awkwardly, like a wrestler struggling to break a hold, he turned inside them.

He saw the face of the girl from the party, very near to his. 'Tip!' he cried. 'God, I'm glad to see you!'

When you came right down to it, Forrester hardly knew the girl, barring a little friendly kissing at a party, but at this moment she was very dear to him. It was like a chance meeting in Taiwan with somebody who had sat at the far end of the same commuter train for years. Not a friend, hardly even an acquaintance; but promoted by the accident of unexpected meeting to the status of near and dear. Half rising from his seat, he hugged her tight. She laughed breathlessly and shook free. 'Dear Charles,' she gasped, 'not so *hard*.'

'I'm sorry.' She sat down opposite him, and he sank back in his chair, admiring her dark hair and pale skin, her cheerful, pretty face, and her figure. The others in the tea room, some of whom had turned to look at them, were losing interest and returning to their own affairs. Forrester said, 'It's just that I'm so glad to see you, Tip.'

She looked startled, then faintly reproving. 'My name is Adne Bensen, dear Charles. Call me Adne.'

'But last night Hara called you—oh!' he said, remembering. 'Then you're the girl who has been sending me the messages.'

She nodded.

'Very nice messages they were,' he said. 'Would you like some tea?'

She said, 'Oh, I think not. I mean, not here, anyway. I came to see if you'd like to come to my place for dinner.'

'*Yes!*'

She laughed. 'You are such an impetuous man, Charles. Is that why they call you the kamikaze people? I mean, your century and all.'

'As to that, Adne, I don't know,' he said. 'Because, when you come right down to it, I don't know who calls me what. I am, you might say, confused. One of the many reasons why I am pleased to see you is that I need somebody to talk to.'

She leaned back in her chair, smiling, and said she would take some tea, after all. It came without being asked for; apparently the joymaker had monitored their conversation and drawn the inferences any good waiter would draw. She threw back her filmy, puffy wrap – it had floated around her shoulders like a cloud, but now it lay back against the chair quite inconspicuously, Forrester noticed – to reveal a deep-cut, tight-fitting, flesh-colored vest or jerkin of some sort, which was startling at first glance.

At the second, it was still startling.

She said, 'Dear Charles. Don't you ask your joymaker things?'

'I would, except I don't know what to ask.'

'Oh, anything! What do you want? Have you filed an interests profile?'

'I don't think so.'

'Oh, do! Then it will tell you what programs are on, what parties you will be welcomed at, who you would wish to know. It's terrible to go on impulse, Charles,' she said earnestly. 'Let the joymaker help you.'

He discovered that his own teacup had been replenished and he took a sip. 'I don't understand,' he said. 'You mean I should let the joymaker decide what I'm going to do for fun?'

'Of course. There's so *much*. How could you know what you would like?'

He shook his head . . .

But that was all of that conversation, all for then. His joymaker said suddenly, its voice curiously tinny, *'Priority urgent! This is a drill! Take cover! Take cover Take cover!'*

'Oh, dear,' said Adne, pouting. 'Well, let's go.'

'Take cover!' blared the joymaker again, and Forrester discovered the reason for its metallic sound. Not only his but the girl's, those of patrons at other tables, all the joymakers at once were repeating the same message. *'Take cover! Countdown starts now! One hundred seconds. Ninety-nine. Ninety-eight.'*

'Where are you going?' Forrester asked, rising with her.

'To the shelter, of course! Hurry it up, Charles, will you? I hate it when I'm out in a public place in one of these things.'

'. . . *Ninety-one. Ninety. Eighty-nine . . .*'

He asked, swallowing hard, 'Air raid? A *war*?'

She held his hand and was tugging him along toward an exit at the rear of the tea room, through which the other patrons were already beginning to stream out. 'Not exactly, Charles dear. Don't you know *anything*?'

'Then what?'

'Aliens. Monsters. That's all. Now hurry, or we'll never get a seat.'

FIVE

A walk, an elevator ride, a short stretch through a light-walled corridor, and they came out into a great shadowy auditorium. There was just enough light to find their way to seats. It was filling rapidly, and behind them Forrester heard heavy doors slamming.

When about three quarters of the seats were filled, a man in black climbed onto the stage and said, 'Thank you all for your cooperation. I'm pleased to be able to tell you that this building has achieved four-nines compliance in exactly one hundred and forty-one seconds.'

There was a stir of interest from the audience. Forrester craned his neck to find the source of the PA system – it seemed to murmur from all over the hall – and located it at last as the man spoke again. It was his joymaker, and all the joymakers, repeating what the man said.

'This is one of the best showings we've ever had,' he said warmly, 'and I appreciate it. You may leave.'

'You mean that's all there is to it?' Forrester asked the girl.

'That's all. Are you coming up to my place?'

'But,' he went on, 'if there's going to be a raid, or any chance of one, shouldn't we wait and see—'

'See what, Charles dear? There's no need to grovel in the ground like *moles*. It's just a test.'

'Yes, but—' He hesitated, and then followed her out of the auditorium thoughtfully.

It was confusing. No one had mentioned war to him.

But when he said as much to Adne, she laughed. '*War*? Oh Charles! You're so *funny*, you kamikazes! Now we've wasted enough time – are you coming to my place for dinner or not?'

He sighed.

'Oh, sure,' he said. As brightly as he could.

In the life that had begun with his birth in 1932 and ended with the inhalation of a lungful of flame thirty-seven years later, Forrester had been a successful, self-sufficient, and substantial man.

He had had a wife – her name was Dorothy – small, blonde, a little younger than himself. He had had three sons, and a job as copy chief of a technical writing service, and a reputation among his friends as a fine poker player and useful companion.

Although he had missed combat participation in a war, he had been a Boy Scout during World War Two, participating in scrap-metal drives and Slap the Jap waste-fat collections. As a young adult he had lived through the H-bomb hysteria of the early fifties, when every city street blossomed out with signs directing the nearest way to a bomb shelter. He had seen enough movies and television shows to know what air raid drills meant.

He was not very satisfied with the one he had just seen. He tried to phrase his dissatisfaction to Adne as she changed clothes behind a screen, but she was not very interested. Drills were an annoyance to her, it was clear, but not a very serious one.

She came out from behind the screen, wearing something filmy and pale and not at all practical for cooking dinner. On the other hand, Forrester thought, who knew how these people cooked their dinners? She rustled over to him, lifted his hand, kissed his fingers, and sat down beside him, pulling her joymaker from the place by the arm of the chair where she had left it. 'Excuse me, Charles dear,' she said; and, to the joymaker, 'Receiving messages.'

Forrester could not hear what the joymaker said to her, because she was holding it close to her ear and had evidently somehow turned the volume down – which he resolved to learn how to do. But he heard what she said to it, although the words were mostly incomprehensible. 'Cancel. Hold Three. Commissary four, two as programmed, two A-varied.' And, 'That takes care of that,' she said to him. 'Would you like a drink?'

'All right.' She lifted glasses out of the well of the— Forrester would have called it a cocktail table, and perhaps it was. He noticed her eyes were on a stack of parcels on a low table across the room. 'Excuse me,' she said, pouring a glass of minty liquid for him and one for herself. 'I just have to look at these things.' She took a small sip of her drink, rose, walked over to the table.

Forrester decided he liked his drink, which was not sweet and made his nose tingle. He stood up and crossed over to her. 'Been shopping?' he asked. Adne was taking out clothes, small packets that might have been cosmetics, some things like appliances.

'Oh, no, Charles dear. It's my job.' She was preoccupied with a soft, billowy green thing, stroking it against her cheek thoughtfully. With a twist of her arms she threw it around her shoulders and it became a sort of Elizabethan ruff. 'Like it, dear?'

'Sure. I mean, I guess I do.'

'It's soft. Feel.' She drew it over his face. It felt like fur, although its points thrust out again the moment they left his skin, looking starched and thorny. 'Or this,' she said, taking it off and replacing it with something that had looked like oiled silk in the box it came in, but which, on her shoulders, disappeared entirely, except that it gave luster and color to her skin. 'Or—'

'They're all beautiful,' he said. 'What do you mean, it's your job?'

'I'm a reacter,' she said proudly. 'Weighted at nearly fifty million, with two-nines reliability.'

'Which means?'

'Oh, you know. If I like a thing, chances are ninety-nine out of a hundred that the others will, too.'

'Fifty million others?'

47

She nodded, flushed and pleased.

'And this is how you make your living?'

'It's how I get rich,' she corrected him. 'Say!' She looked at him thoughtfully. 'I wonder. Do you have any idea how many others like you have come out of the dormers? Maybe you could get a job doing the same thing. I could ask—'

He patted her hand indulgently, amused. 'No thanks,' he said, careful not to mention the fact that he was rich – although, he remembered dimly, he had been far less reticent about it at the party the night before. Well, he had made a lot of mistakes at that party – as witness his troubles with the Martian.

'I never asked,' said Adne, putting the things away. 'How did you die, Charles?'

'Why,' he said, sitting down again and waiting for her to join him, 'I died in a fire. As a matter of fact, I understand I was a hero.'

'Really!' She was impressed.

'I was a volunteer fireman, you know, and there was an apartment fire one night – it was January, very cold, if you stood in the puddles of water you'd freeze to the ground in two minutes – and there was a child in the upper part of the building. And I was the nearest one to the ladder.'

He sipped his drink, admiring its milky golden color. 'I forgot my Air-Pak,' he admitted. 'The smoke got me. Or the combination did – smoke and heat. And maybe booze, because I'd just come from a party. Hara said I must have inhaled pure flame, because my lungs were burned. My face must have been, too, of course. I mean, you wouldn't know, but I don't think I look quite the same as I used to. A little leaner now, and maybe a little younger. And I don't think my eyes were quite as bright blue.'

She giggled. 'Hara can't help editing. Most people don't mind a few improvements.'

Dinner arrived as his breakfast had that morning, through a serving door in the wall. Adne excused herself for a moment while the table was setting itself up.

48

She was gone more than a moment and came back looking amused. 'That's that,' she said without explaining. 'Let's eat.'

Forrester was able to identify few if any of the foods served him. The textures were sort of Oriental, with crisp things like water chestnuts and gummy things like sukiyaki lending variety to the crunch of lettuce and the plasticity of starches. The flavors were queer but palatable. While they ate he told her about himself – his life as a tech writer, his children, the manner of his death.

'You must have been one of the first to be frozen,' she commented. '1969? That's only a few years after it began.'

'First on the block,' he agreed. 'It was because of the fire company, I guess. We'd just got the new death-reversal truck – gift of our local millionaire, who wanted it around. I didn't think I'd be the one to christen it.'

He ate a forkful of something like creamed onions in pastry crust and said, 'It must have been confusing for Dorothy.'

'Your wife?'

He nodded. 'I wonder if there's any way I can find out about her. What she did. How the children made out. She was young when I was killed ... Let's see. Thirty-three, about. I don't know if having a husband dead but frozen ... if she would marry again, ... Hope she did. I mean—' He broke off, wondering what he did mean.

'Anyway,' he said, 'Hara had some records. She lived nearly fifty more years, died in her eighties of the third massive stroke. She'd been partly paralyzed for some time.' He shook his head, trying to visualize small, blonde Dorothy as an ancient, bedridden beldame.

'Had enough?' asked Adne.

He came back to present time, faintly startled. 'Dinner? Why, I guess so. It was delicious.' She did something that caused the table to retract itself and stood up. 'Come over here and have your coffee. I ordered it specially for you. Would you like some music?'

He started to say, 'Not particularly,' but she had already turned on some remote recording equipment. He paused to listen, braced for almost anything, with visions of Bartok and *musique concrète*. But it turned out to be something very like violins, playing something very like detached, introspective Tchaikovsky.

She sank back against him and she was very warm and fragrant. 'We'll have to find you a place to live,' she said.

He put his arm around her.

'This is a condominium building,' she said thoughtfully, 'but I think there might be something. Do you have any preferences?'

'I don't know enough to have preferences.' He caressed her soft hair.

She said drowsily, 'That's nice.' And in the same tone, a moment later, 'But I think I should warn you I'm natural-flow. And this is about M day minus four, so all I want is to be cuddled.' She yawned and touched her mouth with her hand. 'Oh! Excuse me.'

Then she caught a glimpse of his face. 'You don't mind, do you?' she asked, sitting up. 'I mean, I could take a pill – Charles, why are you that color?'

'Nothing. Nothing at all.'

She said apologetically, 'I'm sorry, but I don't know much about kamikaze ways. If there's a ritual taboo . . . I'm sorry.'

'No taboo. Just a misunderstanding.' He picked up his glass and held it out to her. 'Any more of this stuff around?''

'Charles dear,' she said, stretching, 'there's all you want. And I have an idea.'

'Shoot.'

'I'm going to find you a place to live!' she cried. 'You just stay here. Order what you want.' She touched something that he could not see and added, 'If you don't know how, the children will show you while they're keeping you company.'

What had seemed to be a floor-length mural opened itself

50

and became a doorway. Forrester found himself looking into a bright, gay room where two small children were racing each other around a sort of climbable maze.

'We ate our dinner, Mim,' cried one of them, then saw Forrester and nudged the other. The two looked at him with calm appraisal.

'You don't mind this, either, do you, Charles dear?' Adne asked. 'That's another thing about being natural-flow.'

There were two of them, a boy and a girl, about seven and five, Forrester guessed. They accepted him without question ...

Or not exactly that, thought Forrester ruefully. There were questions.

'Charles! Did people really *smell bad* in the old days?'

'Oh, Charles! You rode in *automobiles*?'

'When the little children had to work in the coal mines, Charles, didn't they get anything to *eat*?'

'But what did they *play* with, Charles? Dolls that didn't *talk*?'

He tried his best to answer. 'Well, the child-labor time was over when I lived, or almost. And dolls did talk, sort of. Not very intelligently—'

'When *did* you live, Charles?'

'I was burned to death in 1969—'

The little girl shrieked, 'For *witchcraft*?'

'Oh, no. No, that was hundreds of years earlier, too.' Charles tried not to laugh. 'You see, houses used to catch on fire in those days—'

'The Shoggo fire!' shouted the boy. 'Mrs Leary's cow and the earthquake!'

'Well – something like that. Anyway, there were men whose job it was to put the fires out, and I was one of them. Only then I got caught and died there.'

'Mim drowned once,' the little girl bragged. '*We* haven't died at all.'

'You were sick once, though,' said the boy seriously. 'You could have died. I heard Mim talking to the medoc.'

51

Forrester said, 'Are you children in school?'

They looked at him, then at each other.

'I mean, are you old enough to start lessons?'

The boy said, 'Well, *sure,* Charles. Tunt ought to be doing hers right now, as a matter of fact.'

'So should you! Mim said—'

'We have to be polite to the guest, Tunt!' The boy said to Charles, 'Is there anything we can get you? Something to eat? Drink? Watch a program? Sex-stim? Although I guess you ought to know,' he said apologetically, 'that Mim's natural-flow and—'

'Yes, yes, I know about that,' Forrester said hastily, and thought, Sweet God!

But when in Rome, he thought, it was what the Romans did that counted, and he resolved to do his best. He resolved it earnestly.

It was like being at a party. You got there at ten o'clock, with your collar too tight, and a little grouchy at being rushed and your starched shirt front still damp where the kids had splashed it as you supervised their bedtime tooth-brushing. And your host was old Sam, who'd been such a drag; and his wife Myra was in one of her nouveau-riche moods, showing off the new dishwasher; and the conversation started out about politics, which was Sam's most offensive side . . .

But then you had the second drink. And then the third. Faces grew brighter. You began to feel more at ease. The whole bunch laughed at one of your jokes. The music on the stack of records changed to something you could dance to. You began to catch the rhythm of the party . . .

Oh, I'll try, vowed Forrester, joining the children in a sort of board game played against their own joymakers. I'll catch the mood of this age if it kills me. Again.

SIX

Up betimes, and set out to conquer a world.

The home that Adne found for him was fascinating –
walls that made closets as he needed them, windows that
were not windows but something like television screens – but
Forrester resolutely spent no time exploring its marvels.
After a disturbed night's sleep he was up and out, testing his
new world and learning to cope with it. The children were
marvelous. He begged the loan of them from Adne, and they
were his guides. They took him to the offices of the Nineteenth Chromatic Trust, where a portly old Ebenezer
Scrooge gravely examined Forrester's check, painstakingly
showed him how to draw against it, severely supervised his
signing the necessary documents to open an account, and
only at the end revealed himself by saying, 'Man Forrester,
good day.' They took him to a Titanian restaurant for lunch,
a lark for them, but for him a shattering test of nerve, since
the Titanians ate only live food, and he was barely able to
cope with an aspic that writhed and rustled in his spoon.
They showed him their playschool, where for three hours a
week they competed and plotted with their peers (their
lessons were learned at home, via their child-modified joymakers), and Forrester found himself playing London
Bridge is Falling Down with fourteen children and one other
adult, symbolically acting out the ritual murder and en-
tombment in the bridge's foundations that the nursery
rhyme celebrated. They took him to where the poor people
lived, with half-fearful giggles and injunctions against
speaking to *anyone,* and Forrester found himself out of
pocket change, having given it all away to pale, mumbling
creatures with hard-luck stories about Sol-burn on Mercury
and freezer insurance firms that had gone bankrupt. They

took him to a park – indoors, underground – where the landscaping was topologically grotesque and a purling stream flowed through a hill's base and up the other side, and where ducks and frogs and a feathery sort of Venusian fish ate morsels of food the children tossed them. They took him to a museum where animated enlarged cells underwent mitosis with a *plop* like a cow lifting her foot from a bog, and a re-created Tyrannosaurus rex coughed and barked and thumped its feet clangorously, its orange eyes glaring straight at Forrester. They showed him all their treasures and pleasures. But they did not show him a factory, or an office building, or a store of any size. For it did not seem that any of these existed any more. They showed him all around Shoggo until their joymakers chided them and Forrester's own said severely 'Man Forrester! The children must be returned for their naps. And you really must receive your messages.'

The children looked at him with woe. 'Ah, well,' said Forrester, 'we'll do it again another day. How do we get home from here?'

'A cab,' said the girl doubtfully, but the boy shouted, 'Walk! We can walk! I know where we are – ten minutes will do it. Ask your joymaker if you don't believe me.'

'I believe you,' said Forrester.

'Then this way, Charles. Come on, Tunt.' And the boy led off between two towering buildings on the margin of a grassy strip, where huge hovercraft swished by at enormous speeds.

The joymaker complained, 'Man Forrester, I have dichotomous instructions. Please resolve them.'

'Oh, God,' said Forrester, tired and irritable. 'What's your trouble now?'

'You have instructed me to hold messages, but I have several that are high priority and urgent. Please reaffirm holding order, stipulating a time limit if possible or receive them now.'

The boy giggled. 'You know why, Charles?' he demanded. 'It tickles them when they're holding messages. It's like if you have to go to the bathroom.'

The joymaker said, 'The analogue is inexact, Man Forrester. However, please allow me to discharge my message load.'

Forrester sighed and prepared to contemplate reality again. But something distracted him.

Besides the steady *whush, whush* of the passing hovercraft, besides the distant chant of a choir – they were passing some sort of church – there was another sound. Forrester looked up.

A faint tweeting sound of communications equipment was coming from a white aircraft, glass-fronted, hanging overhead. It bore the shining ruby caduceus, and behind the glass a dark-skinned man in blue was regarding Forrester gravely.

Forrester swallowed.

'Joymaker,' he demanded, 'is that a death-reversal vehicle overhead?'

'Yes, Man Forrester.'

'Does that mean—' He cleared his throat. 'Does that mean that crazy Martian is after me again?'

'Man Forrester,' said the joymaker primly, 'among your urgent priority messages is a legal notice. The twenty-four-hour hold period having expired, and appropriate notices and action having been filed and taken, the man Heinzlichen Jura de—'

'Cut it out! Is he *after* me?'

'Man Forrester,' said the joymaker, 'yes. As of seventeen minutes ago, the hold period having expired then, he is.'

At least the crazy Martian wasn't in sight, thought Forrester, scanning the few visible pedestrians. But the presence of the death-reversal aircraft was a poor omen.

'Kids,' he said, 'we got troubles. I'm being chased.'

'Oh, Charles!' breathed the boy, fascinated. 'Will you get *killed*?'

55

'Not if I can help it. Look. Do you know any short cuts from here? Any secret ways – through cellars, over rooftops – you know.'

The boy looked at the girl. The girl's eyes got very big.

'Tunt,' she whispered, 'Charles wants to *hide*.'

'That's it,' said Forrester. 'What about it, son? You must know some special way. Any kid would.'

The boy said, 'Charles, I know a way, all right. But are you sure—'

'I'm sure, I'm sure!' snapped Charles Forrester. 'Come on! Where?'

The boy surrendered. 'Follow me. You too, Tunt.'

They turned and dived into one of the buildings. Forrester took a last look around for Heinzlichen whatever-his-name-was. He was not in sight. Only the hovercraft thrumming past, and the few uncaring pedestrians ... and overhead the man in blue in the death-reversal vehicle, staring down at him, his expression both surprised and angry.

When he was safely back in the condominium building, the children returned to their own home to await the arrival of their mother. Forrester hurried to his apartment, closed the door, and locked it.

'Joymaker,' he said, 'you were right. I admit it. So now let's have all those messages. And take it slow, so I can understand what they're about.'

The joymaker said serenely, 'Man Forrester, your messages follow. Vincenzo d'Angostura states that he is still available for legal representation, but will not call again under Bar Association rules. Taiko Hironibi feels there was some misunderstanding and would like to discuss it with you. Adne Bensen sends you an embrace. A document package is in your receiving chute. Will you receive the embrace?'

'Hold it a minute. Gives me something to look forward to. Is any of the other stuff important?'

'As to that, Man Forrester, I have no parameters.'

56

'You're a big help,' said Forrester bitterly. 'Get me a drink while I'm thinking. Uh, gin and tonic.' He waited for it to appear and took a long pull.

His nerves began to feel less like tangled barbed wire. 'All right,' he said. 'Now, what was that about a package?'

'You have a document package in your receiving chute, Man Forrester. Envelope. Approximately nine centimeters by twenty-five centimeters, less than one half centimeter in thickness, weighing approximately eleven grams. Inscription: "Mr Charles Dalgleish Forrester, Social Security Number 145–10–3088, last address while living 252 Dulcimer Drive, Evanston, Illinois. Died of burns received October 16th, 1969. To be delivered upon revival." Contents unknown.'

'Hum. Is that all it says?'

'No, Man Forrester. There are machine-script handling instructions on the document. I will phonemize them as closely as possible: "Sigma triphase ooty-poot trip toe, baker tare sugar aleph, paraphrase—" '

'Yeah, well, that's enough of that. I mean, is there anything in English? Anything I could understand?'

'No, Man Forrester. Faint carbonization marks are visible where the envelope has been creased. There are several minor discolorations, which may represent latent human skinprints. At some time a mild corrosive liquid was spilled—'

'Say, joymaker,' said Forrester, 'I've got an idea. Why don't I open it up? Where'd you say it was?'

Retrieved from his receiving chute, the envelope turned out to be a letter from his wife.

He stared at it and felt something tingling in the corners of his eyes. The handwriting was very strange to him. The signature was 'Still with affection, Dorothy' ... but the hand that had formed those letters scrawled and shook. She had even abandoned her little finishing-school affectations of penmanship, the open-circle dots over the *i*'s, the

57

flowing crosses on the *t*'s. He could read it only with difficulty.

Dear Charles,

This is, I think, the tenth or eleventh time I have written this letter to you. I seem to do it every time there is a death or bad news, as though the only gossip I have that is worth the effort to pass on for what may be another century – or more! – is that which has to do with troubles. Not your troubles, of course. Not any more. Usually the troubles are mine.

Although I must say that really my life has not been a burden to me. I remember that you made me happy, Charles. I must tell you that I missed you terribly. But I must also tell you that I got over it.

To begin with: You will want to know what you died of, I know, and perhaps the people who bring you back to life will not be able to tell you. (I am assuming that you will be brought back to life. I didn't believe it at the time – but since then I've seen it happen.)

You were burned to death in a house fire on Christie Street on October 16th, 1969. Dr Ten Eyck, who was with the first aid squad, pronounced you dead and, with some difficulty, persuaded them to use their death-reversal equipment to freeze you. There was some trouble about lacking glycerol for perfusion, but the whole fire company, you will be glad to know, dug into their liquor closets and came up with several bottles of bourbon . . . and it was that which was used as a buffer. (If you woke up with a hangover, you now know why!)

There was some question as to whether too much time had elapsed, too. They thought you might have spoiled during the discussion, you see. But as it was cold weather for October they decided to take a chance, and you were ultimately consigned to a freeze-dormer at liquid helium temperatures. Where, as I write this, you now lie . . . and where, or in one like it, I expect to be myself before long.

I should tell you that I didn't pay for any of this. Your fire company insurance, it turned out, was adequate to cover all the costs and was in fact earmarked for that purpose. If it had been up to me I don't think I would have gone to the expense, Charles, because after all there were the children to bring up.

What can I tell you about them? They missed you very much.

Vance, in particular, played truant from school for the best part of a month, forging notes to his teacher, persuading some adult – I suspected our cleaning woman at the time – to phone the principal to explain his absence, before I found out about it. But then he joined a Boy Scout troop and, as they say, developed other interests.

David didn't say much. But I don't think he ever got over it. At least not during his lifetime. He joined the Peace Corps four years later and was executed by insurgents during the Huk uprising in 1974. Since his body was mutilated before being found he could not be frozen. So he, at least, we will never see again.

Vance is now married, and is in fact a grandfather. It was his second marriage; the first was annulled. His present wife was a schoolteacher before their marriage . . . and they have been happy. And I really can think of nothing else to tell you about your son Vance that does not involve attempting to explain what broke up his first marriage and why his second wife could not stay in the United States. I suppose you may meet him some day. You can ask him yourself.

Billy, you will be astonished to learn, is now a Great Man. Let me see. He was two when you died. Now he's our senator from Hawaii, and they say he will be President one day. But you will find out more about him in the history books than I can tell you, I think. Let me only say, what I know will interest you, that his first campaign was on a platform of free freezing for everyone, paid for out of Social Security funds, and you were mentioned in every speech. He won easily.

And I . . . am seventy-nine years old.

Since you died forty years ago I cannot now remember you well enough, my Charles, to know if you will mind what I have to say next. Three years after your death I remarried. My husband – my other *husband – was a doctor. Still is, though he is out of practice now. We have been very happy, too. We had two other children. Both girls. You never met him, but he is a good man, barring the fact that at one time he drank too much. He gave it up. He looks a little like you ...*

If I remember correctly, he does.

And I am now in brittle health and I think this is the last time I will write you this letter. Perhaps we will meet again. I wonder what it will be like.

Still with affection,
Dorothy

Forrester put down the letter and cried, 'Joymaker! Was there ever a President named Forrester?'

'President of what, Man Forrester?'

'President of the United States!'

'Which United States is that, Man Forrester?'

'Oh, for God's sake! The United States of America. Wait a minute. First off, do you know the Presidents of the United States of America?'

'Yes, Man Forrester. Washington, George. Adams, John. Jefferson, Thomas—'

'Later on! starting with the middle of the twentieth century.'

'Yes, Man Forrester. Truman, Harry S. Eisenhower, Dwight D. Kennedy—'

'Move it up! Start with around 1990.'

'Yes, Man Forrester. Williams, Harrison E. Knapp, Leonard. Stanchion, Karen P. Forrester, Wilton N. Tschirky, Leon—'

'Well, my God,' said Forrester softly, and sat marveling while the joymaker droned on to the end of the twenty-first century and stopped.

Little two-year-old Willy. Baby Bill. A senator ... and President. It was an unsettling idea.

The joymaker said, 'Man Forrester! Notice of physical visit. Adne Bensen is to see you, purpose unstated, time of arrival less than one minute.'

'Oh,' said Forrester, 'good. Let her right in.' And he rehearsed what he would tell her, but not to any effect. Genealogy was not what was on her mind. She was angry.

'You,' she cried, 'what the sweat do you think you're doing to my kids?'

'Why, nothing. I don't know what you're talking about.'

'Dog sweat!' The door crashed closed behind her. 'Twitching kamikaze!' She flung her cape against the wall; it dropped to a chair and arranged itself in neat square folds. 'Pervert creep, you get a kick out of this, don't you? Want to make my kids like you! Want to change them into chatter-toothed, handworking, dog-sweaty, *cowardly*—'

Forrester guided her to a chair. 'Honey,' he said, attempting to get her a drink, 'shut up a minute.'

'Oh, sweat! Give me that—' She quickly produced drinks for them, without a pause in her talking. 'My kids! You want to *ruin* them? You hid from a challenge!'

'Look, I'm sorry, but I didn't mean to get them in a dangerous—'

'Dangerous! Go crawl! I'm not talking about *danger*.'

'I didn't let them get hurt—'

'Sweat!'

'Well, it isn't my fault if some crazy Martian—'

'*Dog* sweat!' She was wearing a skintight coverall that seemed to be made of parallel strands of fabric running top to bottom, held together God knew how; with every movement as she turned, as her breast rose and fell, tiny slivers of skin showed disturbingly. 'You're not even a man! What do you know about—'

'I said I was sorry. Listen, I don't know what I did wrong, but I'll make it up to them.'

She sneered.

61

'No, I *will*! ... I know. There must be something they want. I've got plenty of money, so—'

'Charles, you're pathetic! You haven't got money enough to feed a sick pup – or character enough to make him a dog. Go rot!'

'Now, wait a minute! We're not married. You can't talk to me like that!' He got up and stood over her, the glass unheeded in his hand. Now he was getting angry, too. He opened his mouth to speak, gesticulating.

Six ounces of icy, sticky fluid slopped into her face.

She stared up at him and began to laugh.

'Oh, Charles!' She put down her own glass and tried to wipe her face. 'You know you're an idiot, don't you?' But the way she said it was almost affectionate.

'I'm sorry,' he said. 'Times, let's see, times three, anyway. For spilling the drink on you, for getting the kids in trouble, for yelling back at you—'

She stood up and kissed him swiftly. As she lifted her arms, the strands of fabric parted provocatively. She turned and disappeared into the protean cubicle of the lavatory.

Forrester picked up the rest of his drink, drank it, drank hers, and carefully ordered two more from the dispenser. His brow was furrowed with thought.

When she came back he said, 'Honey, one thing. What did you mean when you said I didn't have a lot of money?'

She fluffed her hair, looking abstracted.

He said persistently, 'No, I mean it. I mean, I thought you knew Hara pretty well. He must have told you about me.'

'Oh, yes. Of course.'

'Well, then, I had this insurance thing when I died, you see. They banked the money or something, and it's had six hundred years to grow. Like John Jones's Dollar, if you know what that was. I didn't have much to begin with, but by the time they took me out of the cooler it was over a quarter of a million dollars.'

She picked up her new drink, hesitated, then took a sip of

it. She said, 'As a matter of fact, Charles dear, it was a lot more than that. Two million seven hundred thousand, Hara said. Didn't you ever look at your statement?'

Forrester stared. 'Two million sev – Two mill—'

'Oh, yes.' She nodded. 'Look it up. You had the papers with you in the tea room yesterday."

'But – but, Adne! Somebody must've – I mean, your kids were with me when I deposited the check! It was only two hundred and some thousand.'

'Dear Charles. Will you please look it up in your statement?' She stood up, looking somewhat annoyed and, he thought, somewhat embarrassed. 'Oh, where the devil did you put it? It was a silly joke anyway, and I'm tired of it.'

Numbly he stood up with her, numbly found the folder from the West Annex Discharge Center, and placed it in her hands. What joke? If there was a joke, he didn't know what it was. But already he didn't like it.

She fished out the sheaf of glossy sheets in the financial report, glanced at them, began handing them to him. The first was entitled CRYOTHERAPY, MAINTENANCE, SCHEDULE 1. It bore a list of charges under headings like Annual Rental, Biotesting, Cell Retrieval and Detoxification, as well as a dozen or more recurring items with names that meant nothing to him – Schlick-Tolhaus Procedures, Homiletics, and so on. On the second sheet was a list of charges for what appeared to be financial services, presumably investing and supervising his capital. The third sheet covered diagnostic procedures; there were several for what seemed to be separate surgeries, sheets for nursing care and for pharmaceuticals used ... There were in all nearly thirty sheets, and the totals at the bottom of each of them were impressive, but the last sheet of all took Forrester's breath away.

It was a simple arithmetical statement:

AGGREGATE OF CONVERTED ASSETS	$2 706 884.72
AGGREGATE OF SCHEDULES 1–27	$2 443 182.09
NET DUE PATIENT ON DISCHARGE	$ 263 702.63

Forrester gasped and coughed and cried, half strangled, 'Two and a half million *dollars* for medical— Sweet Jesus God!' He swallowed and looked up unbelievingly. 'Holy AMA! Who can afford that kind of money?'

Adne said, 'Why, you can, for one. Otherwise you'd still be frozen.'

'Christ! And—' A thought struck him— 'Look at this! Even so they're cheating me! It says two hundred and sixty thousand, and they only gave me two thirty!'

Adne was beginning to look faintly angry again. 'Well, after all, Charles. You did go back there for extra treatment. You might get some of that back from Heinzie, I don't know ... Of course, he's protesting it because you messed things up.'

He looked at her blankly, then back at the statement. He groaned.

'Reach me my drink,' he said and took a long pull of it. He announced, 'The whole thing's crazy. Millions of dollars for doctors! People just can't *have* that much money.'

'You did,' she pointed out. 'Given time, people can. At compound interest, they can.'

'But it's – it's – medical profiteering! I don't know what they did to me, but surely there should be *some* attempt to control fees!'

Adne took his arm and drew him down again on the couch beside her. She said with patience, but not very much patience, 'Dear Charles, I wish you would learn a little something about the world before you tell us all what's wrong with it. Do you know what they had to do to you?'

'Well – Not exactly, no. But I know something about what medical treatment costs.' He frowned. 'Or used to cost, anyway. I suppose there's inflation.'

'I don't think so. I – I think that's the wrong word,' she said. 'I mean, that means things cost more because the money is worth less, right? But that isn't what happened. Those operations would have cost you just as much in the nineteenth century, but—'

'Twentieth!'

'Oh, what's the difference? Twentieth, then. That is, they would have cost just as much if anybody had been able to do them. Of course, nobody was.'

Forrester nodded unwillingly. 'All right, I admit I'm alive and I shouldn't kick. But still—'

Impatiently the girl selected another document from the sheaf, glanced at it, and handed it to him. Forrester looked, and he was very nearly sick. Full color, nearly life size, he thought at first that it was Lon Chaney made up as the Phantom of the Opera.

But there was no makeup. It was a face. Or what was left of one.

He gagged. 'What – What—'

'Do you see, Charles? You were in bad shape.'

'*Me?*'

'Oh, yes, dear. You really must read your report. See here . . evidently you fell forward into the flames. Besides your being killed, the whole anterior section of the head was destroyed. At least, the soft parts. Mm . . . lucky your brains weren't cooked, at that.' He saw with incredulity that this tender, charming girl was studying the photograph with as little passion as though the charred meat it represented were a lamb chop. She went on, 'Didn't you say you noticed your eyes were different? New eyes.'

Forrester croaked, 'Put that thing away.'

He took a swallow of his drink and immediately regretted it, then fished one of the remaining cigarettes out of his second pack and lit it. 'I see what you mean,' he said at last.

'Do you, dear? Good. You know, I bet four or five hundred people worked on you. All sorts of specialists. All their helpers. Using all their equipment. They get a case like yours, it's like one of those great big enormous jigsaw puzzles. They have to put it all back together, piece by piece – only they don't have all the pieces, so they have to get or make new ones . . . and of course the stuff spoils so. They have to—'

'Quit it!'

'You're awfully jumpy, Charles.'

'All right! I'm jumpy.' He took a deep drag on the cigarette and asked the question that had been developing in his mind for ten minutes now. 'Look. At a normal rate of expenditure – oh, you know; the way you see me living – roughly how long is my quarter of a million dollars going to last?'

She looked into space and tapped her fingernails against her teeth. 'There are those custom items of yours,' she said thoughtfully. 'They come high – those things you smoke and fowl eggs, and – what was that other thing? The oransh juice—'

'Leaving out that kind of stuff! How long?'

She pursed her lips. 'Well, it depends—'

'Roughly! How long?'

She said, 'Well, maybe the rest of this week.'

He goggled at her. He repressed a laugh that sounded almost like a sob.

The end of the *week*?

He had been building himself up to hear an answer he wouldn't like, but this exceeded his expectations. He said wretchedly, 'Adne – what am I supposed to do?'

'Well,' she said, 'you could always get a job.'

'Sure,' he said bitterly. 'Got one up your sleeve? One that pays a million dollars a week?'

To his surprise, she seemed to take him seriously. 'Oh, Charles! Not that much. I mean, you're not skilled. Twenty, twenty-five thousand a day – I don't think you can really expect more.'

He said, 'You can find me a job like *that*?'

'Well, what do you think Taiko would have paid?'

'Wait a minute! You mean Taiko would have given me a *job*? But I thought— I mean, he said it was his club. What did he call it, the Ned Lud Society?'

'Yes, that's right.' She nodded. 'What do you think a club's for, Charles?'

'Why – so that people with like interests can, well, get together and work on their interests.'

'And what did you used to so quaintly call a business company?'

'Why . . . Yeah, but look, a company produces something of *value*. Something you can *sell*.'

She sniffed. 'We've got beyond that sort of consideration. Anything that any reasonably competent people agree is worth doing is worth a salary in exchange for doing it.'

'Gosh,' said Charles Forrester.

'But Taiko was quite astonished at the way you acted, Charles. I don't know whether he's angry or not. But I wouldn't count on the offer still being open.'

'Figures,' said Forrester gloomily, musing over lost possibilities.

'Man Forrester!'

The sound of the joymaker was almost like an alarm wakening him from sleep. It took him a few moments to realize what it was, as he emerged from his bemused state. Then he said, 'In a minute, machine. Adne, let me get this straight—'

But she was looking urgent and abashed. 'Charles dear, you'd better take this message.'

'Man Forrester! I have a priority notice of personal visit!'

'Yeah, but Adne—'

'Charles,' she said, 'please take it. Or – never mind. I'll tell you myself.' She looked down at her hands, avoiding his eyes. 'I guess I should have told you before. I think that's Heinzie coming now.'

'Heinzie? The *Martian*? The one—'

She said apologetically, 'I told him to come, Charles dear. You'd really better let him in.'

SEVEN

As Forrester faced the man named Heinzlichen Jura d
Syrtis Major, he felt he was in the state described as 'read
for anything'. What this actually meant was that he wa
totally unready. He did not know what to expect. He coul
feel his heart pounding; he sensed that his hands were be
ginning to shake. Even Adne seemed stimulated; she wa
watching them, her small face intensely interested, and sh
was fumbling something out of her joymaker. A tran
quilizer? No, more likely something to pep her up, though
Forrester. Whatever it was, she popped it in her mouth, and
swallowed before she said, 'Hello, Heinzie. Come on in.
think you and Charles have met.'

Forrester gave her a look, then returned to Heinzlichen
He started to put out his hand, then stopped, balancing o
the balls of his feet, half ready to shake hands, half in
stance resembling the attack position of karate. 'We've met
all right. Too damned often, if you ask me.'

Heinzlichen came in, allowed the door to close behind
him, and stood still, studying Forrester as if he were a speci
men in a museum. Adne had been playing with the light
again, and mottled reds and yellows flecked his face. The
suited his personal color scheme. He was a tall, fat man. Hi
hair was red, and he wore a close-cut red beard that covered
all of his face except for nose, lips, and eyes, like the mask o
a chimpanzee. He rubbed his beard thoughtfully while he
examined Forrester's face with attention, glanced apprais
ingly at his arms and body, stared down at the position o
his feet, and finally nodded. He returned his gaze to a poin
on Forrester's chest and stabbed at it with a finger. He said
'Dat is where I will kill you. Dere. In de heart.'

Forrester exhaled sharply through his nose. It tingled. He

felt the flush of adrenalin through his bloodstream. He opened his mouth; but Adne cut in swiftly before he could speak.

'Heinzie dear! You promised.'

'Promised? What promised? I promised to talk, dat's all. So let's talk.'

'But Charles doesn't understand how things are, Heinzie. Sit down. Have a drink.'

'Oh, sure I'll have a drink. You pick me out something nice. But make it fast, because I have only a couple of minutes.' He returned to Forrester. 'Well? You want to talk?'

Forrester said belligerently, 'You're damned right I want to talk. And, no, Adne, I don't want a drink. Now, look here, you—' He hesitated, finding it hard to think of the right thing to say. 'Well, what I want to know is, why the devil do you want to kill me?'

The Martian looked baffled. He glanced at Adne helplessly, then back to Forrester. 'Sweat, I don't know,' he said. 'Up dere at de party you stomped my foot . . . But I guess I just didn't like you anyway. What do you want to ask a question like dat for?'

'Why? It's my life!'

The Martian growled, 'I knew dis was a bad idea. Honey, I'm going. De more I see of dis guy, de less I like him.'

But Adne had her hand on his arm. 'Please, Heinzie. Here.' She handed him a fizzy orange drink in a thing like a brandy inhaler with a hollow stem. 'You know Charles is just out of the sleep-freeze. He's kind of a slow learner, I'm afraid.'

'Dat's his business. Killing him, dat's my business.' But the Martian grumpily accepted the drink. The girl pressed her advantage.

'Yes, but Heinzie – dear – what's the fun of it if he doesn't know what it's all about?'

'Trimmer!' Heinzlichen growled. 'Maybe it's more fun

dat way. I can't help dinking we lose some of de important values when killing's all so cut and dried.'

'All right, Heinzie, maybe you're right, but there's such a thing as fair play, too. Why, I don't even think Charles really knows what his rights are.'

The Martian shook his head. 'Dat's not my business eider. Dere's his joymaker; let him call up and find out.'

Adne winked reassuringly at Forrester, who was not in the least reassured. But she seemed more confident and relaxed now. She leaned back, sipping her drink, and said silkily. 'Wouldn't it be nicer for you to talk to him about it? Tell Charles what you want to do, exactly?'

'Oh, dat part's all right.' The Martian put down his drink, scratched his beard thoughtfully, and said, 'Well, it's like dis. I want to beat him up good, and den I will stomp on his chest cage until it breaks and ruptures de heart. De reason I like to do it dat way is it hurts a lot, and you don't get near de brain. Of course,' he mused, 'I got to pay a little more, but de best pleasures are de ones you pay for. Cheap's cheap.' Then his expression lightened – or seemed to: the beard hid most of his transient looks. 'Anyway,' he added, 'maybe I can get off paying de bill. I talked to de lawyer, and he said Forrester hasn't touched all de bases, law-wise, so maybe we can fight de costs. But dat doesn't matter in de long run. What de hell, if it costs it costs.'

Forrester nodded thoughtfully and sat down. 'I believe I'll have that drink now, Adne,' he said. He realized, with a certain amount of pride, that he was perfectly calm.

The reason was that Forrester had come to a decision while Heinzlichen was talking: he had decided to go along with the gag. True, it wasn't really a gag. True, when this man said he intended to cause Forrester a lot of pain and bring about his ultimate death, he meant every word of it. But you could not spend your life in weighing consequences. You had to pretend that the chips were only plastic and did not represent real currency of any sort, otherwise you would lose the game out of nerves and panic.

70

The very fact that the stakes were so important to Forrester was a good reason for pretending they were only make-believe.

He accepted a glass from Adne and said reasonably, 'Now, let's get this straight. Did I understand you right? You talked to a lawyer before you tried to kill me?'

'Nah! Wake up, will you? All I did den was file de papers.'

'But you just said—'

'Listen, why don't you? De *papers* was so I could kill you – all de usual stuff, bonds to cover de DR business, guaranties against damaging de brain, and like dat. Den de *lawyer* was just yesterday, when I got de idea maybe I could kill you and save all de bond and guaranty money.'

'Excuse me. I didn't understand that part.' Forrester nodded pleasantly, thinking hard. It began to make a certain amount of sense. The thing you had to remember was that death, to these people, was not a terminal event but only an intermission.

He said, 'As I understand it – I mean, if I understand it – the legal part of this business means you have to guarantee to pay my freezer costs if you kill me.'

'Nah! Not "if." Odderwise you got it.'

'So I don't have anything to say about it. The law lets you kill me, and I'm stuck with it.'

'Dat's right.'

Forrester said thoughtfully, 'But it doesn't sound fair to me, everything considered.'

'Fair? Of course it's fair! Dat's de whole idea of de guaranties.'

'Yes, of course – if the circumstances are normal. But in this case, with death-reversal out of the question ...'

The Martian snorted angrily. 'Are you crazy?'

'No, really,' Forrester persisted. 'You said you were going to try to get out of paying my expenses. You know more about it than I do. Suppose you succeed?'

'Oh, boy! Den you have to pay dem yourself.'

71

Forrester said politely, 'But you see, I can't. I don't have any money to pay them with. Ask Adne.'

The Martian turned to Adne with a look of unbelieving anger, but she said, 'As a matter of fact, Heinzie, Charles is telling you the truth. I didn't think of it, but it's so. I mean, I haven't checked his balance . . . but it can't be much.'

'De hell with his balance! What de sweat do I care about his balance? I just want to kill him!'

'You see, Jura, if you kill me—'

'Shut up, you!'

'But the way things are—'

'Dog sweat!' The Martian's face was working angrily under the mask of beard. He was confused, and that made him mad. 'What's de matter with you, Forrester? Why didn't you get a job?'

'Well, I will. As soon as I can.'

'Sweat! You want to chicken out, dat's all!'

'I simply didn't understand my money situation. I didn't *plan* it this way. I'm sorry, Jura, I really am, but—'

'Shut up!' barked the Martian. 'Look, I got no more time for dis talk. I have to go to de rehearsal hall; we're doing de Schumann *lieder*, and I'm de soloist. Answer de question. Do you want to chicken out?'

'Well,' said Forrester, fiddling with his glass and casting a sidelong glance at Adne, 'yes.'

'Fink! Dog-sweat fink!'

'I know how you feel. I guess I'd feel the same way.'

'De hell with how you'd feel. All right, look. I'm not promising anything, but I'll talk to de lawyer again and see where de hell we stand. Meanwhile, you get a job, hear?'

Forrester showed the Martian out. For some reason that he could not quite analyze, he was feeling elated.

He stood thoughtfully at the door, testing the feeling. For a man who had just discovered he was a pauper, who had reinforced the dislike of an enemy who proposed to kill him, Forrester was feeling pretty good. Probably it was all illusion, he thought fatalistically.

Adne was curled up on the couch, studying him. She had been doing something with the lights again; now they were misty blue, and her skin gleamed through the lacy strands of her coverall. Perhaps she had been doing something with that, too; it seemed to be showing more of Adne than it had earlier. Forrester excused himself and went into the little lavatory room to splash cold water on his face. And then he realized the cause of his elation.

He had managed to win a point.

He was not a bit sure it was a worthwhile point; he wasn't even quite sure of what he had won. But, for better or for worse, he had gained a small victory over Heinzlichen Jura de Syrtis Major. For days Forrester had been a cork bobbling to the thrusts of every passerby; now he was thrusting back. He came smiling back into the room and cried, 'I want a drink!'

Adne was still on the couch, murmuring into her joy-maker. '—And be sure you're locked up,' she was saying. 'Don't forget your prophylaxis and say good night, Mim.' She put it down and looked up at him. Her expression was sulky but entertained.

'The kids?' She nodded. 'My God, is it that late?' He had forgotten the passage of time. 'I'm sorry. I mean, what about their dinners and all?'

She looked slightly less sulky, slightly more entertained. 'Oh Charles! You weren't thinking I had to boil oatmeal or peel potatoes? They've had their dinners, of course.'

'Oh. Well. I guess we should be thinking about ours . . .'

'Not yet.'

Forrester said, reorienting his thinking very quickly, 'All right. Then what about that drink?

'I'm not thirsty, you fool. Sit down.' She lifted her joy-maker, looked him over with narrowed eyes, kissed the soft spot at the base of his throat, and touched it with the joy-maker.

Forrester felt a sudden surge inside him. It was like a mild electric shock, like a whiff of mingled oxygen and musk.

73

Adne studied him critically, then leaned forward and kissed him on the lips.

A moment later he said, 'Do that again.'

She did. Then she lay back against him with her head on his shoulder.

'Dear Charles,' she said, 'you're such a nut.'

He stroked and kissed her hair. The parallel-strand fabric did not feel coarse or wiry; he could hardly tell it was there.

'I don't know if you did the right thing with Heinzie,' she said meditatively. 'It's kind of – you know. Almost chicken . . .' Then she turned inside his arm and kissed his ear. 'I know it embarrasses you when I talk biology, but – well, the reason I'm natural-flow, you see, is that I'm a natural type of girl. Do you understand?'

'Sure,' he lied, only vaguely hearing her.

'I mean, if you want to you can take the pills and use the chemosimulants, and it's just *about* the same. But I don't do that, because, if you're going to do that, you might just as well go all the way and use the joy machine.'

'I can see that, all right,' he said, but she fended him off and added, 'Still, one doesn't have to be *rigid*. Sometimes you're at a low point, and something special happens, and you'd like to be at a high point. Then you can take a pill if you want to, do you see?'

'Oh yes! Say!' said Forrester, pleasantly excited, 'I wonder! How would you feel about taking a pill now?'

She sat up, stretched, and put her arms around him. 'Don't have to,' she said, resting her cheek against his. 'I took one when you let Heinzie in.'

With two victories in one day, thought Forrester in a mood of pleasant triumph and lassitude, this world had come pretty close to his first hopes for it, after all. After the girl had gone; he slept for ten good hours and woke with the conviction that everything would turn out right. The father of a President and the lover of Adne Bensen was, at least in his own eyes, a figure of much mana. There were problems. But he would cope with them.

74

He ordered breakfast and added, 'Machine! How do I go about getting a job?'

'If you will state parameters, Man Forrester, I will inform you as to openings that may be suitable.'

'You mean, what kind of job? I don't know what kind. Just so it pays—' he coughed before he could get the figure out—'around ten million bucks a year.'

But the joymaker took it in stride. 'Yes, Man Forrester. Please inform me further as to working conditions: home or external; mode of payment – straight cash or fringed; if fringe, nature permitted – profit-sharing, stock issue, allocated earnings bonus, or other; categories not to be considered; religious, moral or political objections, not stated in your record profile, which may debar classes of employ—'

'Slow down a minute, machine. Let me think.'

'Certainly, Man Forrester. Will you receive your messages now?'

'No. I mean,' he added cautiously, 'not unless there are some life-or-death ones, like that Martian being out to kill me again.' But there weren't. That, too, thought Forrester with pleasure, set this day off from other days.

He ate thoughtfully and economically, bathed, put on clean clothes, and allowed himself an extremely expensive cigarette before he tackled the joymaker again. Then he said, 'Tell you what you do, machine. Just give me an idea of what jobs are open.'

'I cannot sort them unless you give me parameters, Man Forrester.'

'That's right. Don't sort them. Just give me an idea of what's going.'

'Very well, Man Forrester. I will give you direct crude readout of new listings as received in real time. Marking. Mark! Item, curvilinear phase-analysis major, seventy-five hundred. Item, chef, full manual, Cordon Bleu experience, eighteen thousand. Item, poll subjects, detergents and stress-control appliances, no experience required, six thousand. Item, childcare domestics – but, Man Forrester,' the

75

joymaker broke in on itself, 'that clearly specifies female employment. Shall I eliminate the obviously inappropriate listings?'

'No. I mean, yes. Eliminate the whole thing for now. I get the idea.' But it was confusing, thought Forrester uncomfortably; the salaries mentioned were hardly higher than twentieth-century scale. They would not support a Pekingese pup in this era of joyful extravagance. 'I think I'll go see Adne,' he said suddenly, and aloud.

The joymaker chose to reply. 'Very well, Man Forrester, but I must inform you as to a Class Gamma alert. Transit outside your own dwelling will be interrupted for drill purposes.'

'Oh, God. You mean like an air raid.'

'A drill, Man Forrester.'

'Sure. Well, how long is that going to go on?'

'Perhaps five minutes, Man Forrester.'

'Oh, well, that's not so bad. I tell you what, why don't you give me my messages while I'm waiting.'

'Yes, Man Forrester. There are one personal and nine commercial. The personal message is from Adne Bensen and follows.' Forrester felt the light touch of Adne's hand, then the soft sound of Adne's voice. 'Dear Charles,' her voice whispered, 'see me again soon, you dragon! And you know we have to think about something, don't you? We have to decide on a name.'

EIGHT

When he reached Adne's apartment, the children let him in.
'Hello, Tunt,' he said. 'Hello, Mim.'

They stared at him curiously, then at each other. Blew it
again, he thought in resignation; it must be the girl that's
Tunt, the boy that's Mim. But he had long since decided that
if he tried to track down all his little errors he would have
time for nothing else, and he was determined not to be de-
railed. 'Where's your mother?' he asked.

'Out.'

'Do you know where?'

'Uh-huh.'

Forrester said patiently, 'Would you like to tell me
where?'

The boy and girl looked at each other thoughtfully. Then
the boy said, 'Well, not particularly, Charles. We're kind of
busy.'

Forrester had always thought of himself as a man who
liked children, but, although he smiled at these two, the
smile was becoming forced. 'I guess I can call her up on the
joymaker,' he said.

The boy looked scandalized. '*Now?* While she's *crawling*?'

Forrester sighed. 'Look, fellows, I want to talk to your
mother about something. How do you recommend I go
about it?'

'You could wait here, I guess,' the boy said reluctantly.

'If you *have* to,' added the girl.

'I get the impression you don't want me around. What are
you kids doing?'

'Well—' The boy overruled his sister with a look and said
sheepishly, 'We're having a meeting.'

'But please don't tell Taiko!' cried the girl.

'He doesn't like our club,' the boy finished.

'Just the two of you?'

'Sweet sweat, no!' laughed the boy. 'Let's see. There are eleven of us.'

'Twelve!' the girl crowed. 'I bet you forgot the robot again.'

'Maybe I did. You and me, Tunt. Four boys. Three girls. A grown-up. A Martian . . . and the robot. Yeah, twelve.'

'You mean a Martian like Heinzlichen what's-his-name?'

'Oh, no, Charles! Heinzie's a dope, but he's people. This is one of the big green ones with four arms.'

Forrester did a double take, then said, 'You mean like in Edgar Rice Burroughs? But – but I didn't think those were real.'

The boy looked politely interested. 'Yes? What about it?'

'What do you mean by "real," Charles?' asked the girl.

In the old days, before Forrester died, he had been a science-lover. It had always seemed to him wonderful and exciting that he should be living in an age when electricity came from wall sockets and living pictures from a box on a bench. He had thoughts sometimes, with irony and pity, of how laughably incompetent some great mind of the past, a Newton or an Archimedes, would have been to follow his own six-year-old's instructions about tuning a television set or operating his electric trains. So here I am, he thought wryly, the bushman in Times Square. It's not much fun.

But by careful and single-minded questioning he got some glimpse of what the children were talking about. Their playmates were not 'real,' but they were a lot realer than, say, a Betsy-Wetsy doll. They were analogues, simulacra; the children, when pressed, called them 'simulogs.' The little girl said proudly that they were very good at developing interpersonal relationships. 'Got that much,' said Charles, 'or,

78

anyway, I think I do. So what does Taiko have to do with it?'

'Oh, *him!*'

'He doesn't like anything that's *fun.*'

'He says we're losing the will to cope with – with what you said, Charles. Reality.'

'And all that sweat,' added the girl. 'Say! Would you like to hear him?'

She glanced toward the view-wall, now showing a placid background scene of woody glades and small furry animals. 'You mean on the television?' Forrester asked.

'The what, Charles?'

'On that.'

'That's right, Charles.'

'Well,' said Forrester . . .

And thought that, after all, he might as well. If worst came to worst, he could take up Taiko's offer of a job, assuming it was still open; and before he came to that worst he would be better off knowing something about it. 'Display away,' he said. 'What have I got to lose?'

The viewing wall, obedient to the little girl's orders, washed out the forest glade and replaced it with a stage. On it a man in a fright wig was bounding about and howling.

With difficulty Forrester recognized the blond, crew-cut visitor he had so unceremoniously got rid of – when? Was it only a couple of days ago? Taiko was doing a sort of ceremonial step dance: a couple of paces in one direction and a stomp, a couple of paces away and another stomp. And what he was shouting seemed like gibberish to Forrester.

'Lud, lords, led nobly!' (*Stomp!*) 'Let Lud lead, lords,' (*Stomp!*) 'lest lone, lorn lads lapse loosely, (*Stomp!*) 'into limbo!' (*Stomp!*) He faced forward and threw his arms wide. The camera zoomed in on his impassioned, tortured face. 'Jeez, kids! You want to get your goddamn brains scrambled? You want to be a juiceless jellyfish? If you don't, then – let Lud lead!' (*Stomp!*) 'Let Lud lead!' (*Stomp!*) 'Let Lud lead—'

The boy cried over the noise from the view-walls, 'Now he's going to ask for comments from the viewers. This is where we usually send in things to make him mad, like "Go back in the freezer, you old icy cube" and "Taiko's a dirty old Utopian!" Of course, we don't give our names.'

'Today I was going to send in, "If it was up to people like you we'd still be swinging from our tails like apes," ' said the girl thoughtfully, 'but it probably wouldn't make him very mad.'

Forrester coughed. 'Actually, I'd just as soon not make him mad. I may have to go to work for him.'

The children stared at him, dismayed. The boy extinguished Taiko's image on the view-wall and cried, 'Please, Charles, don't do that! Mim said you turned him down.'

'I did, but I may have to reconsider; I have to get some kind of a job. Matter of fact, that's why I'm here.'

'Oh, good,' said the girl. 'Mim'll get you a job. Won't she, Tunt?'

'If she can,' the boy said uncertainly. 'Say, what can you do, Charles?'

'That's one of my problems. But there has to be something; I'm running out of money.'

They did not respond to that, merely looked at him wide-eyed. They not only looked astonished, they looked embarrassed.

At length the little girl sighed and said, 'Charles, you're so sweaty ignorant I could freeze. I never heard of anybody being out of money, 'cept the Forgotten Men. Don't you know how to get a job?'

'Not very well.'

'You use the joymaker,' the boy said patiently.

'Sure. I tried that.'

The boy looked excited. 'You mean— Look, Charles, you want me to help you? Cause I will. I mean, we had that last year in Phase Five. All you have to do is—'

His expression suddenly became crafty. 'Oh, sweat, Charles,' he said carelessly, 'let me do it for you. Just, uh, tell it to listen to me.'

Forrester didn't need the girl's look of thrilled shock to warn him. 'Nope,' he said firmly. 'I'll wait for your mother to come home.'

The boy grinned and surrendered. 'All right, Charles. I just wanted to ask it something about Mim's other— Well, here's what you do. Tell it you want to be tested for an employability profile and then you want recommendations.'

'I don't exactly know what that involves,' Forrester said cautiously.

The boy sighed. 'You don't have to understand it, Charles. Just do it. What the sweat do you think the joy-maker's *for*?'

And, actually, it turned out to be pretty easy, although the employability profile testing involved some rather weird· questions. . .

What is 'God'?

Are your stools black and tarry?

If you happened to be a girl, would you wish you were a boy?

Assume there are Plutonians. Assume there are elves. If elves attacked Pluto without warning, whose side would you be on?

Why are you better than anyone else?

Most of the questions were like that. Some were worse – either totally incomprehensible to Forrester or touching on matters that made him blush and glance uneasily at the children. But the children seemed to take it as a matter of course, and indeed grew bored before long and wandered back to their own view-wall, where they watched what seemed to be a news broadcast. Forrester growled out the answers as best he could, having come to the conclusion that the machine knew what it was doing even if he didn't. The answers, of course, made no more sense than the questions;

81

tardily he realized that the joymaker was undoubtedly monitoring his nervous system and learning more from the impulses that raced through his brain than from his words, anyway. Which was confirmed when, at the end of the questions, the joymaker said, 'Man Forrester, we will now observe you until you return to rest state. I will then inform you as to employability.'

Forrester stood up, stretched, and looked around the room. He could not help feeling that he had been through an ordeal. Being reborn was nearly as much trouble as being born in the first place.

The children were discussing the scene on the view-wall, which seemed to show a crashed airliner surrounded by emergency equipment, on what appeared to be a mountain top somewhere. Men and machines were dousing it with chemical sprayers and carrying out injured and dead – if they made that distinction – on litters, to what Forrester recognized by the ruby caduceus as death-reversal vehicles. The mountainside was dotted with what looked like pleasure craft – tiny, bright-colored aircraft that had no visible business there, and that seemed to be occupied by sightseers. No doubt they were, thought Forrester – remembering the crowds that had stood by the night he was burned to death, heedless of icy spray, icy winds and irritated police trying to push them back.

'Old Hap's never going to make it,' said the boy to the girl, then looked up as he saw Forrester. 'Oh, you're done?'

Forrester nodded. A drone from the view-wall was saying, '. . . Made it again, with a total to this minute of thirty-one and fifty-five out of a possible ninety-eight. Not bad for the Old Master! Yet Hap still trails the rookie Maori from Port Moresby—'

'What are you watching?' he asked.

'Just the semifinals,' said the boy. 'How'd you make out on your tests?'

'I don't have the results yet.' The screen flickered and

82

showed a new picture, a sort of stylized star map with arrows and dots of green and gold. Forrester said, 'Is ten million a year too much to ask for?'

'Sweat, Charles! How would we know?' The boy was clearly more interested in the view-wall than in Forrester, but he was polite enough to add, 'Tunt's projected life average is about twelve million a year. Mine's fifteen. But of course we've got, uh, more advantages,' he said delicately.

Forrester sat down and resigned himself to waiting for the results. The arrows and circles were moving about the star map, and a voice was saying, 'Probe reports from 61 Cygni, Proxima Centauri, Epsilon Indi, and Cordoba 31353 show no sign of artifactual activity and no change in net systemic energy levels.'

'Dopes!' shrilled the little girl. 'They couldn't find a Martian in a mattress.'

'At Groombridge One, eight, three, oh, however, the unidentified object monitored six days ago shows no sign of emission and has been tentatively identified as a large comet, although its anecliptic orbit marks this large and massive intruder as a potential trouble spot. Needless to say, it is being carefully watched, and SEPF headquarters in Federal City announce that they are phasing two additional monitors out of their passive orbits. . . .'

'What are they talking about?' Forrester asked the boy.

'The war, of course. Shut up, won't you?'

'. . . Well, there's good news tonight from 22H Camelopardis! A late bulletin just received from sortie-control headquarters states that the difficult task of replacing the damaged probe has been completed! The first of the replacements rushed out from BO 7899 has achieved stellar orbit in a near-perfect almost circular orbit, and all systems are go. Seven back-up replacements—'

'Sweat,' said the girl. 'What a tedious war! Charles, you used to do things better, didn't you?'

'In what way?'

The girl looked puzzled. 'More *killing,* of course.'

'If you call that better, maybe we did. World War Two killed twenty million people, I think.'

'*Weep.* Twenty *million,*' breathed the girl. 'And so far we've killed, what is it, Tunt? Twenty-two?'

'Twenty-two million?' asked Forrester.

The boy shook his head disgustedly. Twenty-two individual Sirians. Isn't that rotten?'

But before Forrester could answer, his joymaker spoke up.

'Man Forrester! Your tests have been integrated and assayed. May I display the transcript on Bensen children equipment?'

'Go ahead,' the boy said sullenly. 'Can't be any worse than *that.*'

The star map disappeared from the wall and was replaced by shimmering sine waves, punctuated with numbers that were quite meaningless to Forrester. 'You may apply for re-evaluation on any element of the profile, if you wish. Do you wish to do this, Man Forrester?'

'Hell, no.' The numbers and graphs were not only meaningless but disturbing. Forrester had a flash of memory, which he identified as dating from the last time a government agency had concerned itself with finding him a job – after his discharge from his post-Korean peacetime army service, when he joined the long lines of unemployables telling their lies to a bored State Employment Service clerk. He could almost see the squares of linoleum on the floor, the queues of those who, like himself, wanted only to collect unemployment insurance for a while, in the hope that during that time the world would clarify itself for them.

But the joymaker was talking.

'Your profile, Man Forrester, indicates relatively high employability in personal-service and advocative categories. I have selected ninety-three possible openings. Shall I give you the list?'

'My God, no. Just give me the one you like best.'

'Your optimum choice, Man Forrester, is as follows: Salary, seventeen thousand five hundred. This is rather less than your stated requirements, but an expense—'

'Hold on a minute! I'll say it's less! I was asking for ten million!'

'Yes, Man Forrester. You stated ten million per year. This is seventeen thousand five hundred per day. At four-day-week norm, allowing for projected overtime as against health losses, three million eight hundred thousand dollars per year. Expenses are also included, however, optimized at five million plus in addition to salary.'

'Wait a minute.' The numbers were so large as to be dizzying. He turned to the children. 'That's almost nine million a year. Can I live on that?'

'Sweat, Charles, sure, if you want to.'

Forrester took a deep breath.

'I'll take it,' he said.

The joymaker did not seem particularly concerned. 'Very well, Man Forrester. Your duties are as follows: Conversation. Briefing. Discussion. The orientation is timeless, so your status as a recent disfreezee will not be a handicap. You will be expected to answer questions and be available for discussions, usually remote due to habitat considerations. Some travel is indicated.'

'*Sweat*.' The Bensen children were showing signs of interest; the boy sat up, and his sister stared wide-eyed at Forrester.

'Supplementary information, Man Forrester: This employer has rejected automated services for heuristic reasons. His desideratum is subjectivity rather than accuracy of data. The employer is relatively unfamiliar with human history, culture, and customs—'

'It *is*!' cried the girl.

'—And will supplement your services with TIC data as needed.'

Forrester cut in, 'Never mind that. Where do I go for my interview?'

'Man Forrester, you have had it.'

'You mean I've got the job? But – but what do I do next?'

'Man Forrester, I was outlining the procedure. Please note the following signal.' There was a mellow, booming chime. 'This will indicate a message from your employer. Under the terms of your employment contract, you may not decline to accept these messages during the hours of ten hundred to fourteen hundred on working days. You are further required to receive such messages with no more than twelve hours' delay even on nonworking days. Thank you, Man Forrester.'

And that, thought Forrester, was that.

Except for trying to find out what was bugging the kids. He said, 'All right. What's eating you?'

They were whispering together, their eyes on him. The boy stopped long enough to ask, 'Eating us, Charles?'

'Why are you acting like that?' Forrester amended.

'Oh, nothing.'

'Nothing *important*,' corrected the girl.

'Come on!'

The little girl said, 'It's just that we never knew anybody who'd work for *them* before.'

'Work for who?'

'The joymaker told you, Charles! Don't you listen?' said the boy, and the girl chimed in, 'Sweat, Charles! Don't you know who you're working for?'

Forrester took a deep breath and glared at them. He told himself that they were only children and that in fact he was rather fond of them; but they seemed on this particular morning to be determined to drive him mad. He sat down and picked up his joymaker. Carefully he scanned the cluster of buttons until he found the crystal-clear, rounded one he was looking for, turned the joymaker until its spray nozzle was pointing at the exposed flesh of his arm, and pressed the button.

Happily it was the right button. What the fine mist that danced into his wrist might be he did not know, but it achieved the expected effect. It was like a supertranquilizer; it cleared his mind, quieted his pulse, and enabled him to say, quite calmly, 'Machine! Just who the hell have you got me working for?'

'Do you wish me to display a picture of your employer, Man Forrester?'

'You damn bet I wish!'

'Please observe the view-wall, Man Forrester.'

And observe it Forrester did; and he swallowed hard, stunned.

In all justice to the joymaker, Forrester was forced to admit that he had placed no restrictions on its choice of an employer for him. He had been willing to accept almost anything, but all the same he was surprised.

He hadn't expected his employer to have bright green fur, or a diadem of tiny eyes peering out of a ruff around a pointed head, or tentacles. He had not, in fact, expected it to be one of the enemy, the race whose presence in space had scared mankind into a vast series of raid drills, weapons programs, and space probes . . . in short, a Sirian.

NINE

Forrester could have carried on his new duties anywhere. But he didn't want to, he wanted to return to the nest; and there in his room he wrestled with the joymaker and the view-wall and emerged with some sort of picture of what the Sirians were and what they were doing on Earth.

There were eleven of them, as it turned out. They were neither tourists nor diplomats. They were prisoners.

Some thirty years earlier, the first human vessels had made contact with the outposts of the Sirian civilization – a civilization much like the human in the quality of its technology, quite inhuman in terms of the appearance of its members and in their social organization. The human exploring party, investigating an extrasolarian planet, had encountered a Sirian ship nosing about a ringlike structure orbiting that planet.

Forrester, having learned that much, had already discovered some enormous gaps in his knowledge. Why hadn't somebody said something to him about men exploring extrasolar space? Where was this system? And what was the orbital ring? It puzzled and confused Forrester; evidently it was not a Sirian structure and it certainly was not man's. But he avoided the proliferation of questions in his mind and stuck to the straight line of the first encounter with the Sirians.

The Earth ship was loaded for bear. Having found bear, it pushed all the buttons. The commander may or may not have been given discretion about the chances of alien contact and what to do when and if it happened. But he wasted no time in contemplating choices. Everything the Earth ship owned lashed out at the squat, uneven Sirian vessel – lasers and shells, rockets and energy-emitting decoys to confuse and disrupt its instruments. The Sirians didn't have a chance. Except for a few who were found still alive in space tanks – their equivalent of suits – they all died with their ship.

The Earthmen brought them warily aboard, then turned tail and fled for home. (Years later, remote-operated probes cautiously returned to look at the scene. They discovered that even the wreckage of the Sirian ship was gone, apparently retrieved by . . . someone. Whereupon the probes fled, too.)

Fourteen Sirians had survived the attack. Eleven of them were still alive and on Earth.

Forrester, watching the picture-story of the Sirians spread across his view-wall while the joymaker stolidly recited the facts of their exile, could not help feeling a twinge of sympathy. Thirty years of imprisonment! They must be getting old now. Did they hope? Did they despair? Were their wives and kiddies waiting back in the nest, or hatching pond, or burrow?

The joymaker did not say; it said only that the Sirians had been thoroughly studied, endlessly debated – and released. Released to house arrest.

The Parliament of Ridings had passed laws about the Sirians. First, it was, from that moment, cardinal policy to avoid contact with their home planet. It was possible that the Sirians would not attack even if they discovered Earth – but it was certain that they wouldn't if they didn't. Second, the Sirians now in captivity could never go home. Third – mankind prepared for the attack it hoped would not come.

So the Sirians were spread across the face of the earth, one to a city. They were provided with large subsidies, good living quarters, everything they could want except the freedom to leave and the company of their kind. Every one of them was monitored – not with a mere joymaker. Transponders linked to the central computing nets were surgically built into their very nervous systems. The whereabouts of each was on record at every moment. They were informed as to the areas forbidden to them – rocket landing grounds, nuclear power stations, a dozen other classes of installations. If they ignored the warning, they were reminded. If they failed to heed the reminder, they got a searing jolt of pain in the central nervous system to emphasize it. If that did not stop them, or if for any reason their transponders lost contact with the central computer, they would be destroyed at once. Three of them already had been.

At that moment the mellow chime sounded, the view-wall flickered and changed its picture, and Forrester was face to face with his employer.

It was just like the picture he had seen before. Maybe it was the same Sirian. But it was looking at him now, or seemed to be, although it was hard to tell from the dozens of tiny eyes that rimmed its upper parts, and it spoke to him.

'Your name,' it said in hollow, unaccented English, 'is Charles Dalgleish Forrester, and you work for me and you call me S Four.'

It sounded like a robot talking. More like a robot than the joymaker itself.

'Right, S Four,' said Forrester.

'You tell me about yourself.'

It sounded like a reasonable request. 'All right, S Four. Where do you want me to begin?'

'You tell me about yourself.' The tentacles were rippling slowly, the circlet of tiny eyes winking at random like the lights on a computer. He had been wrong about its sound, Forrester decided. It was more like a dubbed-in voice in a foreign film on the Late Show – back when there were foreign films and Late Shows.

'Well,' said Forrester ruminatively, 'I guess I can start with when I was born. It was the nineteenth of March, nineteen thirty-two. My father was an architect, but at that time he was unemployed. Later he worked as a project supervisor for the WPA. My mother—'

'You will tell me about WPA,' interrupted the Sirian.

'It was a government agency designed to relieve unemployment during the Depression. You see, at that time there were periodic cyclic imbalances in the economy—'

'You will not lecture me,' interrupted the Sirian, 'and will explain terms for which letters WPA are function of entity.'

Dashed, Forrester tried to put in concrete terms the business of the New Deal's work relief program. Only concrete terms would do. The Sirian was distinctly not interested in Forrester's digressions into economic theory. Probably he liked his own theories better. But he seemed interested in, or at least did not interrupt, a couple of jokes about leaf-raking and about a WPA worker falling down when someone kicked the broom he was leaning on. The Sirian listened impassively, the girdle of eyes twinkling, for half an hour by the clock; then it said, cutting through Forrester's description of his high school graduation, 'You will tell me more at another time,' and was gone.

And Forrester was well enough pleased. He had never talked to a Sirian before.

Although the children were romantically thrilled, Adne did not approve when she heard about it. Not in the least. 'Dear Charles,' she said patiently, 'they're the *enemy*. People will say you are doing an evil thing.'

'If they're so dangerous, why aren't they in concentration camps?'

'Charles! You're acting kamikaze again!'

'Or why isn't there a law against working for them?'

She sighed and nibbled what looked like a candied orchid, regarding him with fond concern. 'Oh, Charles. Human society is not merely a matter of *law*. You have to remember *principle* .There are certain standards of what is good and what is bad, and civilized people comply with them.'

Forrester grumbled, 'Yes, I understand that. It's good when anybody jumps on me. It's bad when I try to do anything about it.'

'Kamikaze, Charles! I'm *simply* trying to point *out* to you that Taiko – for instance – would pay you at least as much as this filthy Sirian for a socially *useful* job—'

'Sweat Taiko!' shouted Forrester, making her laugh with his malaprop anger. 'I'm going to do this by myself!'

So Adne left him there on friendly terms, but she left him nonetheless; an engagement in connection with her employment, she said, and Forrester did not know enough about her job to question it. He hadn't found an opportunity to ask what her 'crawling' date had been, nor did he see a chance to bring up her suggestion about picking a name. She volunteered nothing, and he was just as well pleased.

Besides, he wanted to talk more with the children.

With their help he was learning more about the Sirian than the Sirian would be able to learn about him. The kids frothed with information. It wasn't difficult to master all the facts they had on tap, for there were not many real facts about Sirians to learn. All the hostages on Earth were of the same sex, for example, but there was a good deal of argument about what that sex was. Nor was their family structure at all clear. Whatever their relationships may have been on the planet from which they came, none of them had ever given any signs of being particularly depressed over being separated from their near and dear. Forrester took in the information grudgingly; he could not help thinking there should have been more of it. He said, 'Do you mean to tell me that the only time we've ever seen them is this one time when we wiped out their exploring party?'

'Oh, no, Charles!' The boy was indulgent with him. 'We long-range spied their home planet once, too. But that's dangerous. Anyway, that's what they say; so they stopped it. If it was up to me I would have kept it up.'

'And like in the chromosphere of Mira Ceti,' added the girl brightly.

'The what?'

The boy chortled. 'Oh, yeah. That was a fun one! We had it on our class evaluation trip.'

'Sweat!' cried the girl excitedly. 'Say! Maybe Forrester would like to go with us if we do it again. *I'd* like to!'

Forrester felt a sensation of committing himself to more than he liked. He said uncertainly, 'Well, sure. But I don't have much time right now. I mean, these are my working hours—'

'Oh, sweat, Charles,' said the boy impatiently, 'it doesn't take *time*. I mean, you don't go anywhere in *space*. It's a construct.'

'Only it was kind of real, too,' added the girl.

'But it's all just tapes now,' explained the boy helpfully.

'Show him!' crowed the girl excitedly. 'Mira Ceti! Please, Tunt, you *promised!*'

The boy shrugged, cocked an eye thoughtfully at Forrester, then leaned forward. He spoke into his junior joy-maker and touched a button on his teaching desk.

At once the cluttered children's room disappeared, and they were surrounded by a wall of hot swirling gray and incandescent orange. It cleared . . .

And at once Forrester and the two children were seated in the bridge of a spaceship. The toys were gone, the furnishings replaced by bright metal instruments and flickering, whistling gauges. And outside crystal panels surged the devastating chromosphere of a sun.

Forrester shrank back instinctively from the heat before he realized that there was none. It was illusion. But it was perfect.

'By God!' he cried admiringly. 'How does that work?'

'Sweat, *I* don't know,' scoffed the boy. 'That's ninth-phase stuff. Ask your joymaker.'

'Well, machine? How about it?'

The calm voice of the joymaker replied at once. 'The phenomenon you are currently inspecting, Man Forrester, is a photic projection on a vibratory curtain. An interference effect produces a virtual image on the surface of an optical sphere with the nexus of yourself and your companions as its geometric center. This particular construct is an edited

93

and simplified reproduction of scansion of a Sirian exploration vessel in a stellar atmosphere, to wit—'

'That's enough,' interrupted Forrester. 'I liked the kid's answer better.'

But the boy said tautly, 'Knock it off, Charles. We're starting! See, there's this Sirian high-thermal scout vessel, and we're about to run into it.'

A harsh male voice rasped, 'Tractor ship Gimmel! Your wingmate has an engine dysfunction! Prepare to lock, grapple, and evacuate crew!'

'Are!' cried the boy. 'Start search procedures, Tunt – Keep a watch, Charles!' His hands flashed over the keyboard – it had not been there a moment before, but it was operative; when he energized a circuit, their make-believe ship responded. He put it through a turn; the 'virtual' sunship heeled sharply and sped through fountains of flaming gas.

Forrester could not repress his admiration at the perfection of the illusion. Everything was there, everything but the heat and the feeling of motion – and, gazing at the images around him, Forrester could almost feel the surge and shudder of their ship as it responded to the boy's touch at the controls. Clearly, they were part of a squadron on some adventurous, unspecified mission. Forrester saw nothing that resembled a Sirian; he saw nothing at all, in fact, but the serpents and coils of gas through which they hurtled. But he was conscious of illusory vessels around them. A spatter of command signals came through the speaker as other 'ships' talked back and forth. A panel showed their position in plan and elevation as they swam through the stripped-atom gases of Mira Ceti's ocean of fire. Forrester ventured to say, 'Uh, Tunt. What am I supposed to be doing again?'

'Just use your eyes!' the boy hissed, his attention riveted to the controls. 'Don't mix me up, man!' But his sister was shrieking, 'I see it! I see it, Tunt! Look over there!'

'Oh, sweat,' he groaned in despair. 'Will you *ever* learn to make a report?'

She gulped. 'I mean, wingmate sighted, vector oh, seven, oh, I guess. Depression – um – not much.'

'Prepare to grapple!' roared the boy.

Through the incandescent swirl a fat slug of a ship appeared, vanished, and appeared again. It was black against the blinding brilliance of its surroundings. Black on its metal skin, black in its ports, black even at the tail where a rocket exhaust discharged dark gases into the brightness around them. The rocket cut off as a labored voice gasped through the speaker, 'Hurry it up, Gimmel! We can't hold out much longer!'

They jockeyed close to the stranded 'ship', buffeted this way and that by the force of the flaming gas. Forrester stared open-mouthed. There was the ship, derelict and helpless. And beyond it, swimming faintly toward them through the chromosphere, something that was bright even in this explosion of radiation, something that loomed enormous and fearsome . . .

'Holy God,' he cried, 'it's a Sirian!'

And the whole picture shivered and winked away.

They were back in the children's room. For a moment Forrester was almost blind; then his strained optic centers began to register again. He saw the view-walls, the furnishings, the children's familiar faces. The expedition was over.

'Fun?' demanded the girl, jumping up and down. 'Wasn't it, Charles? Wasn't it fun?'

But her brother was staring disgustedly at a read-out on his desk. 'Tunt,' he grumbled, '*you* should know better. Don't you see the tally? We were late locking up. There was a crew of three there, and two of them are scored dead . . . and we never even got to see the Sirian at all. Just *him*.'

'I'm sorry, Tunt. I'll look better next time,' the little girl said repentantly.

'Oh, it's not you.' He glared past her at Forrester and said bitterly, 'They set the norms for a three-person mission. As if *he* was any help.'

Thoughtfully Forrester picked up the mace of his joy-maker, selected a button, pointed it at the base of his skull just behind the ear, and squirted. He was not sure he had picked the right joy-juice for the occasion; what he wanted was something that would make him tranquil, happy, and smart. What he got was more like a euphoric, but it would serve.

He said humbly, 'I'm sorry I messed it up for you.'

'Not your fault. Should have known better than to take you, anyway.'

'But I wish we'd seen the Sirian,' said the little girl wistfully.

'I think I did. A big bright ship? Coming toward us?'

The boy revived. 'Really? Well, maybe that's not so bad, then. You hear that, monitor?' He listened to what was, to Forrester, an inaudible voice from his teaching machine, then grinned. 'We got a tentative conditional,' he said happily. 'Take it again next week, Tunt. For record.'

'Oh, wonderful!'

Forrester cleared his throat. 'Would you mind telling me exactly what it was we just did?' he asked.

The boy put on his patient expression. 'It was a simulated mission against the Sirian exploring party in the chromosphere of Mira Ceti. I thought you knew that. Basically a real observation, but with the contact between our ships and theirs variably emended.'

'Oh. Uh-huh.'

The boy looked quizzically at him. He said, 'The thing is, Charles, we get graded on these simulations. But it's all right; it didn't hurt us.'

'Sure.' Forrester could feel the beginnings of an idea asserting themselves. No doubt it was the spray from the joy-maker, but . . . 'Could you do the same trick with some other things about the Sirians? So I could get a better look at them? Maybe the original encounter, for instance?'

'Neg.' The boy glared at his sister. 'It's Tunt's fault, of

course. She cried when the Sirians got killed. We have to wait to take the prebriefing over when we're older.'

The little girl hung her head. 'I was sad,' she said defensively. 'But there's other things we can do, Charles. Would you like to see the coconut on the Moon?'

'The what?'

'Oh, sweat. We'll just show you.' The boy scratched his ear thoughtfully, then spoke to his junior joymaker. The view-walls clouded again.

'It's supposed to be another artifact like the one the Sirians were searching for in Mira Ceti's atmosphere,' he said over his shoulder, manipulating his teaching machine as he spoke. 'Don't know much about it, really. It's not Sirian. It's also not ours. Nobody knows whose they are, really, but there are lots of them around – and the Sirians don't seem to know any more about them than we do. They're *old*. And this is the nearest one.'

The view-walls cleared to show the lunar Farside. They were near the terminator line, with crystalline white peaks and craters before them, the jet black of a lunar night to one side. They were looking down into the shallow cup of a crater, where figures were moving.

'This is just tape,' the boy said. 'No participation. Just look as long's you want to.'

There was a clump of pressure huts in the crater. Perhaps they were laboratories, perhaps housing for the scientists or for those who were studying the 'artifact' in the center of the screen – or who had been studying it once, perhaps, and had given it up.

It did indeed look like a coconut. As much as it looked like anything.

It was shaggy and rather egg-shaped. Its tendrils of – whatever they were – were not organic, Forrester thought. They were almost glassy in their brightness, reflecting and refracting the sunlight in a spray of color. By the scale of the huts, the thing appeared to be about the size of a loco-motive.

'It's empty, Charles,' volunteered the girl. 'They all are.'

'But what *are* they?'

The girl giggled. 'If you find out, tell us. They'll make us twelfth-phase for sure!'

But the boy said kindly, 'Now you know as much as anybody does.'

'But the Sirians must—'

'Oh, no, Charles. The Sirians are late arrivals. Like us. And that thing's been there, just the way it is now, for no less than a couple of gigayears.' He switched off the scene. 'Well,' he said brightly. 'Anything else you want to know?'

There was indeed. But Forrester had grasped the fact that the more he got to know, the more he was going to realize how little that knowledge was.

Astonishingly enough, it had not really occurred to him before this that a lot of things had been happening to the human race while he was lying deep in the liquid-helium baths of the West Annex Facility. It was like a story in a magazine. You turn a page. Ten years have passed; but you know perfectly well that they weren't *important*; if they were, the author would have told you about them.

But far more than ten years had passed. And they were important, all right. And there was no Author to fill in the gaps in his knowledge.

TEN

On the third day of his job, Forrester had been six days out of the freezer. He felt as though it had been a million.

But he was learning. Yes, he told himself – gravely gratu-latory – he was doing all his homework, and it was only a question of time until all answers were revealed to him and he took his proper place in this freemasonry of heroes.

Meanwhile, working for the Sirian was not at all disagree-able. The social pressure against his job came only from Adne, and he had seen very little of her since that first day. He missed her; but he had other things on his mind. The Sirian – it had agreed to allow Forrester to think of it as a male, although it did not concur in the diagnosis and would not explain further – was curious, insatiable but patient. When Forrester could not answer questions, it permitted him to take time to look them up. Its orientation, surprisingly enough, was all to the past. It volunteered an explanation for this – well, a sort of explanation. In its view, it said, the present state of any phenomenon was a mere obvious deriv-ative of some prior state; and it was the prior states of man-kind that it wanted to know about.

It crossed Forrester's mind that if *he* were a war captive on a planet of alien enemies, the sort of knowledge that he would try to acquire would have more to do with arms and defense strategies. But he was not a Sirian, and he had de-cided not to bother trying to think like one. That was obvi-ously beyond his powers. So he answered questions about Madison Avenue ad agencies and the *angst* that surrounded a World Series, and every day called up his bank to verify that his day's salary had been deposited.

It had finally penetrated to Forrester that money was still money. His quarter of a million dollars would have bought him – and in fact *had* bought him – something very like a quarter of a million dollars' worth of goods and services, even by twentieth-century standards. It was not the dollar that had been inflated. It was the standard of living.

There were so many things that a dollar could now buy . . . And he had been buying quantities of them.

He could even, he discovered, have managed to live out his life on that quarter of a million dollars – just as he could have in 1969 – provided he had lived at a 1969 level. No robot servants. No extensive medical services – above all, no use of the freezer facilities and their concomitant organ banks, prostheses, antientropic chemical flushings and so forth. If he had eaten no costly, custom-prepared natural foods, had not traveled, had acquired no expensive gadgets . . . if he had, to be exact, lived exactly the life of a twentieth-century suburban peasant, he could have made it last.

But not now. It was gone now. All gone, except for a few tens of thousands left in the account at the Nineteenth Chromatic, plus what the Sirian paid to his account every day. It was about enough to pay his standard joymaker fees for a couple of weeks, maybe. If he was careful.

But Forrester was resigned to the situation. He didn't mind it particularly – at least, he didn't mind his bankruptcy, since it lay within his power to work and make more money than he had ever dreamed of anyway. What he minded very much was the fact that he had been a joke – he and his quarter of a million dollars. And he minded most of all the fact that Adne had shared in that joke.

Because dimly, like a faint, predawn glow in the desert, he could see the foretaste of a time when Adne could be very important to him.

Was already very important to him, he thought wryly. At least in a potential sort of way. He wondered again what she had meant about that business of choosing a name . . . and why, he suddenly thought, had she not called him?

But what was important to him, Forrester realized, was not necessarily important to anyone else. For now, he was a

100

sort of apprentice to life. For now, he would wait, and work, and learn. For now he would not push his luck.

Forrester had learned modesty, if he had learned nothing else.

Forrester had not yet discovered that, in one particular and quite unpleasant way, he was on his way to becoming the most important man in the world.

What mostly confused Forrester about his Sirian employer was that the creature seemed preoccupied. Forrester even asked his joymaker about it.

'Can you clarify your question, Man Forrester? What is there about the behavior of Alphard Four Zero-zero Trimate that puzzles you?'

'Just call him "the Sirian", will you? Anyway, he has a funny way of talking.'

'Perhaps that lies in my computation, Man Forrester. The Sirian language is tenseless and quasi-Boolean. I have taken the liberty of translating it into approximately twentieth-century English modes of speech, but if you wish I can give you a more literal rendering or—'

'No, it's not that. He seems to have something on his mind.'

There was a pause of a second or two. Even Forrester knew enough to remark this occurrence; for the computer facilities to hesitate or search for an answer meant that the problem was something remarkable. But all the joymaker said was, 'Can you give me an instance, Man Forrester?'

'Not really. Well, he has me doing some odd things. Is it right for him to want to hypnotize me?'

A pause again. Then the joymaker said, 'I cannot say, Man Forrester. But I advise you to be cautious.'

Well, cautious he was, Forrester reflected. But he was also puzzled.

The Sirian did not repeat its suggestion about hypnotizing Forrester – 'to secure in-depth referents, plus buried traumas of former time' – but it remained hard to figure out. It capriciously had him talking about the twentieth century at one moment, explaining the Arian-Athanasian wars of nearly two millennia before that at another. (Forrester had had to beg time out to research the heresies revolving around the distinction between the words 'homoousian' and 'homoiousian'; even so, he never really did get the problem straight.) It kindly volunteered to assume his joymaker costs as part of his expenses. It refused to allow him to charge as travel expenses a trip to the deepest vaults of Shoggo, where he had been looking up records of the abandoned pressure-dome settlements on Saturn. 'Capricious' was the word.

It occurred to Forrester that the Sirian might simply be lonesome. But it rejected his offer to come visit it in its quarters. And, as far as he was able to tell, it showed no interest in the fate of its ten compatriots also in exile on Earth.

'You explain common-law marriage.' And, gamely, Forrester tried to describe to a Sirian the drives of sexual impulse and family needs, which had brought about a formal institution to regularize irregular conduct. 'There exist trading stamps!' boomed the hollow, empty voice; and Forrester did his best to clarify the complexities of retail supermarket sales. 'You have or have not violated legislative compulsion programs,' stated the Sirian; and that was the most prolonged session of all. Try as he would, Forrester could not seem to get across the idea of a personal ethic – of laws that one did not violate, because they were morally right, and of laws that everyone violated if they possibly could, because they were morally irrelevant.

He found himself feeling sorry for the Sirian. Its homework was even more arduous than his own.

But Forrester's homework could not be neglected. He ordered his joymaker to display the records of the long-range reconnaissance of the Sirian planet.

He had been thinking of the Sirians as a paper tiger, but now he saw fangs. Englobed by fortresses, with fast and mighty vessels of war flitting about like wasps, the whole Sirian system was a vast network of armament. There were a dozen planets in all, two of them in Trojan orbit with Sirius B, the rest normal satellites of the great white star. All were inhabited. All were defended.

Earth's reconnaissance drones had been lucky enough – or unlucky enough – to find themselves observing and taping what seemed to be war games. The Sirians took their war games seriously. Edited and compressed, the records showed a waste of creature and armament that only a massive war effort could justify. A hundred of the great ships were damaged, some destroyed. A fleet of them converged on an icy satellite of one of the outlying planets . . . and the satellite was melted into glowing slag before Forrester's eyes.

There was no more after that. Clearly, the operators of the drones had felt that enough was enough; it was less dangerous to leave the Sirians unwatched than to run the risk of attracting attention with the drones.

Forrester did not again offer to visit the Sirian in its quarters.

On the fifth day of his new life, Forrester arose to the promptings of his bed, ordered a standard low-cost breakfast (it was, as a matter of fact, far tastier than his hand-hewn specials), checked his messages, and started to work.

With some pride in his expertise, he commanded the joymaker to select and mark a course to the buried vastnesses of the American Documentation Institute. The green-glowing arrows sprang to life at his feet. He followed them out the door, into a sort of elevator cab (but one that moved laterally as well as up and down), out of the cab, into another building, through a foyer clattering with old-fashioned punch-card sorters, into a vault containing some centuries-old records in which his employer had shown a certain interest.

His joymaker said abruptly, 'You will inform me about the term "space race".'

Forrester took his eyes from the old microfilm viewer. 'Hello, Sirian Four,' he said. 'I'm busy looking up the beginnings of the Ned Lud Society, as you asked me. It's pretty interesting, too. Did you know they used to break up computers and—'

'You will discontinue Ned Lud Society research and state motives that led two areas of this planet to compete in reaching the Moon.'

'All right. In a minute. Just let me finish what I'm doing.'

There was no answer. Forrester shrugged and returned to the viewer. The Luddites appeared to have taken themselves a great deal more seriously when they first started: where Taiko postured and coaxed, his predecessors had done the Carrie Nation bit with the axes, chopping up computing machines with the war cry, 'Men for men's jobs! Machines for bookkeeping!'

As he read he forgot about the call from his employer. Then—

'Man Forrester!' cried his joymaker. 'I have two urgent notices of intention for you!'

It was the master computing center this time, not the deep, remote, echoless voice of the Sirian. Forrester groaned. 'Not again!'

'Heinzlichen Jura de Syrtis Major—'

'I knew it,' Forrester muttered.

'—states that he has reactivated his hunting permit. You are notified, Man Forrester, so please be guided accordingly.'

'I'm guided, I'm guided. What's the other one?'

'Man Forrester, it is from Alphard Four Zero-zero Trimate,' said the joymaker; then, unbending slightly, 'or, as you call him, Sirian Four. A notice to terminate employment. Guarantees are met, and notice paid. Reason: failure to comply with reasonable request of employer, to wit, research questions concerning early U.S. and U.S.S.R. space probe motivation.'

Forrester squawked, 'Wait a minute! That sounds like – you mean – hey! I'm fired!'

'Man Forrester,' said the joymaker, 'that is correct. You are fired.'

After the first shock had worn off, Forrester was not particularly sorry, although his feelings were hurt. He had thought he was doing as good a job as could be done. Considering the job. Considering the employer.

Nevertheless, it had had its disadvantages, including the barely polite remarks Adne and the children had been passing about working for the enemy. So with a light heart Forrester dismissed the Sirian from his mind and informed the joymaker he wanted another job.

Quite rapidly he had one: standby machine monitor for the great sublake fusion generating station under Lake Michigan. It paid very well, and the work was easy.

Not for twenty-four hours did Forrester discover that the premium pay was due to the fact that, at unpredictable intervals, severe radiation damage was encountered. His predecessor in the job – in fact, all of his predecessors – were now blocks of low-temperature matter in the great lakeside freezers, awaiting discovery of a better technique for flushing the radioactive poisons out of their cells; and the joymaker candidly informed him that their probable wait for thawing and restoration, which depended on the pace at which certain basic biophysical discoveries were likely to be made, was estimated to be of the order of magnitude of two thousand years.

Forrester blew his top. 'Thanks!' he grated. 'I quit! What the devil do they need a human being down here for anyway?'

'In the event of cybernetic failure,' said the machine promptly, 'an organic overseer may retain the potential of voice connection with the central computing facility, providing an emergency capability—'

'It was only a rhetorical question. Forget it. Say,' said

105

Forrester, punching the elevator button that would bring him up to the breather platform at the lake's surface and thence back to the city, 'why didn't you tell me this job would kill me?'

'Man Forrester,' said the machine gravely, 'you did not ask me. Excuse me, Man Forrester, but you have summoned an elevator. Your relief is not due for three hours. You should not leave your station unattended.'

'No, I shouldn't. But I'm going to.'

'Man Forrester! I must warn you—'

'Look. If I read the plaque on the surface right, this particular installation has been in service for like a hundred and eighty years. I bet the cybernetic controls haven't failed once in all that time. Right?'

'You are quite correct, Man Forrester. Nevertheless—'

'Nevertheless my foot. I'm going.' The elevator door opened; he entered; it closed behind him.

'Man Forrester! You are endangering—'

'Oh, shut up. There's no danger. Worst that would happen would be that it might stop working for a while. So power from the city would come from the other generators until it got fixed, right?'

'Yes, Man Forrester, but the danger—'

'You argue too much. Over and out,' said Forrester. 'Oh, except one thing. Find me another job.'

But the joymaker didn't.

Time passed, and it still didn't. It didn't speak to him at all.

Back in his room, Forrester demanded of the joymaker, 'Come on, what's the matter? You computers don't have human emotions, do you? If I hurt your feelings I'm sorry.'

But there was no answer. The joymaker did not speak. The view-walls would not light up. The dinner he ordered did not appear.

The room was dead.

Forrester conquered his pride and went to Adne Bensen's

106

apartment. She was not there, but the children let him in. He said, 'Kids, I've got a problem. I seem to have blown a fuse or something in my joymaker.'

They were staring at him, bemused. After a moment Forrester realized he had blundered in on something. 'What is it, Tunt? Another club meeting? How about it, Mim?'

They burst out laughing. Forrester said angrily, 'All right. I didn't come here for laughs, but what's the joke?'

'You called me Tunt!' the boy laughed.

His sister giggled with him. 'And that's not the worst, Tunt. He called me Mim! Charles, don't you know *anything?*'

'I know I'm in trouble,' Forrester said stiffly. 'My joymaker doesn't work anymore.'

Now their stares were round-eyed and open-mouthed. 'Oh, *Charles!*' Obviously the magnitude of the catastrophe had overwhelmed their defenses. Whatever it was that had been occupying their minds when he came in, they were giving him their whole attention now.

He said uncomfortably, 'So what I want to know is, what went wrong?'

'Find out!' cried Mim. 'Hurry, Tunt! Poor Charles!' She gazed at him with compassion and horror, as at a leper.

The boy knew what practical step to take – at least, he knew enough to be able to find out what Forrester had done wrong. Through his pedagogical joymaker, the boy queried the central computing facilities, listening with eyes wide to the inaudible response, and turned to stare again at Forrester.

'Charles! Great sweat! You quit your job without notice!'

'Well, sure I did,' said Forrester. He shifted uneasily in his seat. 'All right,' he said, to break the silence. 'I did the wrong thing, huh? I guess I was hasty.'

'Hasty!'

'Stupid,' Forrester amended. 'I'm sorry.'

'Sorry!'

'If you just keep repeating everything I say,' said Forrester, 'you might drive me crazy, but you won't be exactly helping me. I goofed. All right. I admit it.'

The boy said, 'Yes, Charles, but didn't you know you forfeited your salary? And you didn't have anything much else, you know. A couple K-bucks sequestrated for the freezers, but not much loose cash. And so you're—' The boy hesitated, forming the words with his lips. 'You're *broke*,' he whispered.

If those were not the most frightening words Forrester had ever heard, they certainly were well up in the running. Broke? In this age of incredible plenty and high-velocity spending? He might as well be dead, again. He sank back in his chair, and the little girl sprang helpfully forward and ordered him a drink. Forrester took a grateful swallow and waited for it to hit him.

It didn't hit him. It was, of course, the best the girl could get for him on her own joymaker, but it had about as much kick as lemon pop.

He put it down carefully and said, 'See if I've got this straight. I didn't pay my bills, so they turned off the joymaker. Right?'

'Well, I guess you could say that.'

'All right.' Forrester nodded. 'So the first thing I have to do is reestablish my credit. Get some money.'

'Right, Charles!' cried the girl. 'That'll fix everything up!'

'So how do I do that?'

The two children looked at each other helplessly.

'Isn't there anything I can do?'

'Well, sure, Charles. Sweat, there's got to be! Get another job, I guess.'

'But the joymaker wouldn't get me one.'

'Sweat!' The boy gazed thoughtfully at his joymaker, picked it up, shook it, then put it down again. 'That's bad. Maybe when Mim comes home she can help you.'

'Really? Do you think she'll help?'

'Well, no. I mean, I don't think she'd know how.'

'Then what do I *do*?'

The boy looked worried and a little scared. Forrester was pretty sure he looked the same way himself. Certainly that was how he felt.

Of course, he told himself, Hara might help him once more; certainly he'd had the practice. Or Taiko might be sportsman enough to get over his snub and reopen the invitation to work for the Luddites.

But he was pretty sure that neither of these possibilities represented any very hopeful facts.

The little girl wandered thoughtfully away, not looking at Forrester, and began muttering into her joymaker – back to the game he had interrupted, Forrester thought with totally unjustified bitterness. He knew it was unjustified. These were only children, and he had no right to expect them to handle adult problems that at least one adult – himself – couldn't handle at all. The boy said suddenly, 'Oh, one other thing, Charles. Mim says Heinzie's out after you again.'

'Don't I know it.' But it didn't seem such a threat, compared with the disaster of insolvency.

'Well, you see, you've got a problem there,' the boy said. 'If you don't have your joymaker you won't have any warning when he's around. And also there's something about the DR equipment you might not know. You have to have *some* credit rating or they won't freeze you at all if you're killed. You know. There's always the chance that you'll do something that annuls the bonds, so Heinzie, or whoever, might protest payment – then they'd be in trouble. I mean, they don't want to get stuck with a stiff that can't pay up.'

'I appreciate their difficulty.'

'I just thought you'd like to know.'

'Oh, you were right.' Forrester's glance wandered. 'Mim – whatever your name is. You! What are you doing?'

The girl looked up from her joymaker, her face flushed with excitement. 'Me, Charles?'

'Yeah. Didn't I hear you mention my name just now?'

'Sure, Charles. I was proposing you for membership in our club. You know, we told you about it.'

'Nice of you,' said Forrester bitterly. 'Has it got a dining room?'

'Oh, it's not that kind of a club, Charles. You don't understand. The club will *help* you. Already they've made a suggestion.'

He looked skeptical. 'Is that going to help?'

'Sweat, yes! Listen. Tars Tarkas just said, "Let him seek in the dead sea bottoms and the ancient cities. Let him join the haunted hosts of old Jasoom." '

Forrester puzzled over the message drearily. 'It doesn't mean anything to me,' he said.

'Of course it does! Clear as the crawlers on the Farside coconut, don't you see? He thinks you ought to hide out with the Forgotten Men!'

ELEVEN

It was only ten minutes' walking from the children's home to the great underbuilding plazas and warrens where the Forgotten Men lived. But Forrester had no guide this time, nor was there a joymaker to display green arrows to guide him, and it took him an hour. He dodged across an avenue of grass between roaring hovercraft, his life in his hands, and emerged under a hundred-story tower where a man came humbly toward him. He looked vaguely familiar.

'Stranger,' the man said, softly pleading, 'Ah've had a turrible lahf. It all started when the mahns closed and my wahf Murry got sick—'

'Buddy,' said Forrester, 'have *you* got a wrong number.'

The man stepped back a pace and looked him up and down. He was tall, lean, and dark, his face patient and intelligent. 'Aren't you the fellah Ah panhandled with those two little kids?' he said accusingly. 'Gave me fifty bucks, Ah think.'

'You remember good. But that was when I had money; now I'm broke.' Forrester looked around at the tall buildings and the greensward. They did not seem hospitable. 'I'd be obliged to you,' he added, 'if you'd tell me where I can sleep tonight.'

The man glanced warily around, as if suspicious of some kind of trick, then grinned and stuck his hand out. 'Welcome to the club,' he said. 'Name's Whitlow. Jurry Whitlow. What happened?'

'I got fired,' said Forrester simply, introducing himself.

Jerry Whitlow commiserated. 'Could happen to anybody, Ah guess. You know, Ah noticed you didn't have a joymaker, but Ah didn't think much about it. Figured, sweat,

111

he's just a damn greenhorn, prob'ly forgot to take it with him. But you got to get yourself one raht away.'

'Why?'

'Whah? Sweat, man! Don't you know you're fur game for anybody on the hunt? They come down here, take one look around, and they see you're busted – hell, man, you wouldn't last out the day.' He unclipped his own joymaker – or what Forrester had taken to be a joymaker – and proudly handed it over. 'Fake, see? But it looks lahk the real thing. Fool anybody. Fooled you, Ah bet.'

It had, as a matter of fact. But actually, Forrester saw with surprise, it wouldn't fool anyone at all, not at close range. It was far too light to be a joymaker, apparently whittled out of some organic plastic and painted in the pale patterns of a joymaker. 'Of course, it don't *work*.' Whitlow grinned. 'But on the other hand Ah don't have to pay rent on it. Keeps 'em off pretty good. Didn't have that, one of these preverts that get they kicks from total death'd come down here and tag me first thing.'

Gently he pulled it out of Forrester's hand and looked at him calculatingly. 'Now, you got to get one just lahk it and, damn, you hit lucky first tahm. Theah's a fellow two houses over makes them to sell. Friend o' mahn. Ah bet he'll give you one for – hell! Maybe little as a hundred dollars!' Forrester started to open his mouth. 'Maybe even eighty! ... Seventy-fahv?'

'Whit,' said Forrester simply, 'I haven't got a dime.'

'Sweat!' Whitlow was awed. Then he shrugged. 'Well, hell, Ah guess we can't let you get killed for a lousy fifteen bucks. Ah'll get you fixed up on spec.'

'Fifteen?'

Whitlow grinned. 'That's without mah commission. Come on with me, boy. You got some ropes to learn!'

The Forgotten Men lived on the castoffs of the great world overhead, but it did not seem to Forrester that they lived badly. Jerry Whitlow was not fat, but he was obviously not starving, either. His clothes were clean and in good repair, his attitude relaxed. Why, thought Forrester, it might even turn out that I'll like it here, once I learn my way around . . .

Whitlow was a first-rate teacher, even though he never stopped talking. He conducted Forrester through under-building mazes and footbridges Forrester had not even seen, his mouth going all the while. Mostly it was the story of his life.

'. . . Laid off at the mahns when Ah was sixteen. Out of work, Chuck, and me with a family to support. Well, we made out, kahnd of, until mah wahf Murry got sick and we had to go on the relief. So a gov'ment man came around and put me on the Aydult Retraining and gave me tests and, Chrahst, Chuck, you know Ah scored so hah Ah just about broke the scales. So then Ah went back to school and—'

He stopped and glanced apprehensively overhead. They were between buildings, under a tiny square of open sky. He grabbed Forrester and dragged him swiftly back into the cellar where the joymaker-maker had kept his shop.

'Watch out!' he whispered fiercely. 'They's a reporter up there!'

The word meant nothing to Forrester, but the tone carried the message. He ran one way, Whitlow the other. The joy-maker-maker's shop had been in a sort of vermiform appen-dix to the plumbing of an apartment complex, in an area where some installation had been designed into the plans, then was outmoded and removed, and the space left vacant. The little man who sold the joymakers occupied a sort of triplex apartment – three rooms on three levels – and out of it and around it ran, for some reason, a net of empty, four-foot-wide tunnels. Down one of them Whitlow fled. Down another ran Forrester.

It was dark. The footing uneven. But Forrester hurried down it, stooped over to avoid banging his head, until the blackness was total and he fell to the rough floor, gasping.

He still did not know what he had been running from, but

Whitlow's fear was contagious. And it reawakened a hundred old pains; until this moment he had almost forgotten the beating he had taken the first day out of the freezer, but the exertion made every dwindling ache start up again. His sides pounded, his head throbbed.

He had now been a Forgotten Man for exactly two hours.

Time passed, and the silence was as total as the darkness. Whatever it was that Whitlow had feared, it did not seem to be pursuing here. It would take a human stoat to pursue a human rabbit in this warren, he thought; and in the darkness maybe even the rabbit would develop claws. It had been bad enough when all he had to fear was the crazy Martian. Now . . .

He sighed, and turned over on the rough, cast-stone floor.

He wondered wistfully what had become of all the furnishings and gadgets he had bought so recklessly for the apartment he no longer owned. Shouldn't there be some sort of trade-in allowance?

But if there was, he did not have the skill to claim it. Nor did he own a working joymaker to help him with instructions. He wondered if Hara would help him out at this last juncture and resolved to go looking for the doctor. After all, it was in a way Hara's responsibility that he was in this predicament . . .

'No,' said Forrester in the darkness, aloud and very clearly.

It wasn't Hara's responsibility at all. It was his own.

If there was one thing that he had learned in his two hours as a Forgotten Man, it was that there were no responsibilities anymore that were not his own. This was not a world where a protective state provided for its people. It was a world of the individual; he was the captain of his fate, the master of his soul—

And the prisoner of his failings.

By the time he heard Whitlow cautiously calling his name, Forrester had come to terms with the fact that he was all alone in a cold and uncaring world.

Cautiously they tiptoed out of the pipes, across a hover-way, and under a huge building that was supported on a thousand elliptical pillars, set in beds of grass. What light kept the grass growing came from concealed fixtures in the ten acres of roof over their heads.

Whitlow, regaining the appearance of confidence, led the way to one particular pillar that held a door, marked in glittering red letters EMERGENCY EXIT. He pushed it open, shoved Forrester inside, and closed it behind them.

'Whew,' he said cheerfully. 'That was close, but we're all raht now. You beginning to get hungry?'

Forrester had been about to ask questions, but that totally diverted his attention. 'Yes!'

Whitlow grinned. 'Figured,' he said. 'Well, Ah've got just the thing for you, prob'ly. Ah've got a steady clah'nt in this building, fellow who used to work with me at the labs, back before. He's on diet programming now, see, and he always manages to slip me something out of the expurimental allowance. So let's see—'

He rummaged in a cupboard and emerged with a pair of thermal-covered hot dishes. They opened at a touch and displayed a steaming, fragrant dinner for two. 'Damn, he done better than ever! Looks lahk smoked oysters Milanese! Sink your teeth in this, Chuck: Ah guarantee you won't do better at the Senate of the Twelve Apostles!'

While he wolfed down the food, Forrester glanced about him to discover what sort of place he was in. It seemed to be an air-raid access to the underground park from the building above, no longer used because, since the beginning of the Sirian threat, complete new facilities had been excavated at the five-hundred-foot subterranean level. But this little forgotten vestige of a completely stocked shelter remained, and, as no one else had any use for it, Whitlow had taken it for his own. It was temperature controlled; it had lights and plumbing; and as Forrester had already seen, it was provided with food storage facilities. All Whitlow had to do was furnish the food. Forrester leaned back, relaxed, trying to

115

summon up the energy to eat a chocolate mousse and half listening to Whitlow's stream of talk. '. . . So then when Ah got out of M. Ah. T. they weren't vurry many jobs open for coal-mahning engineers, of course. So Ah went back and took mah master's in solid-state electronics. Then Bell Labs sent they recruiter up to scout out prospects and he made me this offer, and Ah went into the labs at nahn thousand to start. Sweat, man, things looked *good*. Murry was puttin' on weight, and the kids were fahn. But Ah'd had this little cough for some tahm, and—'

'Whit,' said Forrester, 'hold off on that a minute, will you? I want to ask you something. Why did we hide from that reporter?'

Whitlow looked startled. 'Ah'm sorry,' he apologized after a minute. 'Ah keep forgetting what a greenhorn you are. You don't know about these reporters.'

'No, I don't.'

'Well, all you have to know is seeing one of them's *poison*. Whah, that lahk a vulture hovering over a hill. You just know they's going to be a corpsc down below. See, they've got this Freedom of the Press thing, so when anybody takes out a killing lahcense he got to tell the reporters raht away. And he's got to fahl a complete plan of action, see, so the reporters can be raht there when the blood starts flahing, because they tape it all and they put it on the view-walls. Specially if the killer's in one of the tournaments. Fella from the National Open was here last week and, God, they was reporters hanging out of every cloud.'

'I think I understand,' said Forrester. 'You mean if you can keep out of the way of the reporters, you can probably keep out of the way of the assassins, too.'

'Stands to reason, don't it?'

'I don't know what stands to reason,' Forrester said humbly. He was beginning to wish he had not been so quick to follow the advice of Adne's children, so reluctant to wait and expose himself to more of Adne's gentle scorn. He felt a quick surge of anger. How dare this world treat *his* life so lightly!

But if it had not been for this world he would not have a life at all; would have stayed dead with a lungful of smoke and fire, centuries before, his body now no more than a soft place in the ground. He leaned back and let himself be lulled by Whitlow's continuing story of his own adventures.

'So then Ah went to the comp'ny doctor and he told me Ah had it, all raht. The Big C. Well! Scared? But we had this comp'ny freezer plan at the labs, and Ah reported in to the medics. "Sheeoot," they said. "Lung cancer, hey? Well, you lay raht down here and we'll freeze your bones—" '

Relaxing, half listening, Forrester found himself getting drowsy. It had been a very strange day, he thought; but then he stopped thinking and fell asleep.

In order to live successfully as a panhandler, you had to exercise special care in picking your 'clients,' Whitlow said. The worst thing you could do was guess wrong. There was always the chance that you might sidle up to somebody and hit him for a touch – and then find out that he was some jet-set happy-boy looking for an economical murder to commit, one that might get him out of the problem of paying for the victim's repairs, and one with double thrills, since there was always the chance that the victim would stay dead.

To avoid that, you had to study each prospective mark carefully. No one came down here on business. The best ones were the rubberneck tourists. They usually came in pairs, and, of any two, the one who was being shown around could safely be figured for a greenhorn – himself too fresh out of the freezers, or back from the starways, to be eager for murder as yet. The problem there was to make an accurate assessment of the one who was doing the showing. 'That's whah 'ah picked you, Chuck. Ah wasn't worried about the little boy. Though you can be vurry surprised sometahms.'

And, of course, everything they did was more or less illegal, so you had to watch out for the coppers.

The coppers would not trouble you unless they saw you actually breaking the law – or unless you were wanted for something. Then they would trouble you a lot. Forrester's first contact with one of the coppers came as he was on the point of bracing a woman alone, Whitlow hiding behind a flowering lilac bush and coaching him in whispers. 'See thur, Chuck, what she did? Threw away a cigarette butt. Well, that's ten to one she's from nahnteen eighty or earlier, so go get 'er, boy!' But Forrester had taken no more than a single step before Whitlow's piercing whisper stopped him. *'Copper!'*

The copper was seven feet tall, uniformed in blue, swinging what looked like a nightstick but was not. Forrester had been warned: it was a sort of joymaker, full of anesthetic sprays and projectile weapons. And the copper had seen him.

It strolled right up to them, swinging the stick. It stopped and looked Whitlow in the eyes, right through the lilac blooms. 'Good morning, Man Whitlow,' it said courteously and moved on to Forrester. It stared silently into his eyes. Then, 'Nice day, Man Forrester,' it said, and moved away.

'How'd he know?' gasped Forrester.

'Retina pattern. Don't worry about it; if he wanted you for anything he'd have you by now. Just give him a minute to get out of saht.'

The woman prospect was gone then. But there were plenty of others.

Keeping out of the way of coppers, trying to learn Whitlow's skill at estimating the potentials of a mark, Forrester found that the time passed. Nor was it the most disagreeable way he had even spent a day. The weather was warm and dry, the growing plants were scented, the people he hit up were no worse than the average run. Forrester took five dollars from a pretty girl in a sort of mirror-bright bikini,

118

then fifty from a man who had brought his pet animal – it was a little silk-furred monkey – down to the underbuilding park to run free, and who seemed to accept Forrester's touch as a form of rent for the use of the premises. Forrester paid back Whitlow's outlay for the fake joymaker and found himself with cash money in his pocket. As he could see no particular need for spending much of it, he began to feel solvent again.

Then Whitlow's hawk eyes brightened, and he whispered tautly, 'Eeow! Look over thur, will you? We've got ourselfs a lahv one now!'

On the fringe of a bed of tall gladioli a man had stepped out of a hovercar and dismissed it. He seemed young, although you couldn't really tell. He moved idly across the grass, like a sightseer. His gait was peculiar, and he wore an expression of grave joy as he minced toward them.

'Look how he walks!' exulted Whitlow.

'I am looking. What about it?'

'Whah, Chuck, he's out of low-gee! Thur's a fella just back from a long trip if Ah ever saw one, and prob'ly loaded with pay. Sic 'im!'

Forrester accepted Whitlow's diagnosis unquestioningly. He marched up to the spaceman and said clearly, 'My name is Charles D. Forrester, and due to my ignorance of the customs of this time I've lost all my money and have no work. If you could possibly spare me some cash, I would be deeply indebted to you.'

Whitlow appeared magically at his elbow. 'That goes for me, too, boss,' he said sorrowfully. 'We both in pretty bad trouble. If you could be kahnd enough to help us now, we'd be eternally grateful.'

The man stopped, his hands in his pockets, neither surprised not disturbed. He turned to face them with grave interest. 'Sorry to hear that, gentlemen,' he said. 'What seems to be your problem, sir?'

'Mahn? Well, it's just about lahk Forrester here. Mah name's Whitlow, Jurry Whitlow. It starts way back when Ah was first born, working in the mahns in West Virginia. They closed down, and—'

The spaceman was not only polite but patient. He listened attentively through all of Whitlow's long story, and to as much of Forrester's as Forrester thought worth telling. He commiserated with them, wrote their names down, and promised to look for them again if he ever came back this way. He was, in short, an ideal prospect – not only a spaceman, but a member of one of the rotating crews who manned the right-angle communications satellites that whirled out around the sun at ninety degrees to the ecliptic, furnishing interference-free relay facilities for the whole solar system. The job paid well, but that was only part of it. Because of the energy budget for matching orbits with the right-angle satellites, the crews were relieved only at six-month intervals, and they came back with a fortune in their pockets and a mad hunger for company; and Whitlow and Forrester walked away from him with two thousand dollars apiece.

That night they ate their dinner in a restaurant. Over Whitlow's protests, Forrester insisted on standing treat.

The restaurant was a hangout for Forgotten Men – and Forgotten Women. It was something like a private home, something like an Automat. You had full joymaker service in it, but in order to make it work you had to feed money into a slot. The prices caused Forrester's scalp to prickle, but he reassured himself that he was just learning the ropes and experience was worth paying for; so at Whitlow's suggestion they started with a squirt of joy apiece (fifty dollars a shot), then cocktails (forty), then a clear, filling soup (twenty-five), then more drinks, and about then Forrester began to lose count. He remembered something that looked like meat but wasn't – it seemed to be coated with a sort of vanilla fudge, although it was bloody inside – and then they began drinking in earnest.

They were not alone. The place was crowded. Whitlow seemed to know everyone there, an assembly that hailed

120

from six centuries, seven continents, and one or two extra-terrestrial planets and moons.

There was a huge red-faced man named Kevin O'Rourke na Solis Lacis, who gave Forrester a shock until they exchanged names, for he resembled Heinzie the Assassin. The reason was good, when Forrester found it out: they were both Martians. O'Rourke, however, was a poet. As a matter of principle, he refused to accept the bribes of what he called the iron-headed state. Probing, Forrester discovered that he was talking about foundation grants, which were available to poets in almost any quantity; but O'Rourke spurned them all. He had been briefly involved with the Ned Lud Society – but they were as bad as the iron-heads, he declared. All Earth was a disaster area. Let the Sirians take it away! 'So why don't you go back to Mars?' Forrester inquired, politely enough; but the Martian took it as an insult, glowered, and lumbered away across the room.

'Don' worry 'bout heem,' said the pretty little dark girl who had somehow come to be leaning against Forrester's shoulder, helping him drink his drink. 'He be back. *Certainement.*'

There was a certain United Nations quality to the gathering, Forrester was discovering. Apart from a few oddballs like the Martian poet, the bulk of the Forgotten Men seemed to come from nearly his own time. Had the hardest time fitting in, he supposed – and the hardest time earning money.

But it was not always that. The tiny dark girl, for instance, had originally been a ballet dancer from Czechoslovakia, shot as a Chinese Bolshevik counter-revolutionary in 1991, frozen at great peril by the Khrushchevite underground, revived, killed seven times since in one way or another, and revived each time. Her reasons for hiding out with the Forgotten Men had nothing to do with money – she was loaded, Whitlow whispered; had made a collection of gold and gems from admirers in a dozen countries, over the centuries, and owned them with their pyramiding value now. But one of

121

her assassinations had produced some cell changes in the brain, and now she awoke each time convinced that Stalinist agents lurked abroad, waiting for her. She did not exactly fear them. She objected to the idea of being killed somewhat as Forrester, in the old days, had objected to going to the dentist: you didn't really *worry* about it, but you were pretty sure it would be unpleasant. As someone who had seen each of seven centuries, Forrester found her fascinating – and she was beautiful as well. But she quickly became so drunk that her reminiscences stopped making sense.

He got up for another drink and found himself lurching slightly. Only slightly, he was sure; but somehow, when he got the drink, it spilled all over a lean, old, nearly bald man, who grinned and nodded and said, *'Tenga dura, signore! È precioso!'*

'You're right,' said Forrester, and sat down beside him. Whitlow had pointed him out as they entered, as a sort of curiosity; he had actually been born before Forrester himself. He had been a hundred and seven years old when, in 1988, he had died of an embolism. The embolism could have been repaired at once, but the ravages of age could not. Not then. After six centuries in the dreamless, liquid-helium sleep, his original stake had multiplied to the point where the trustees of the freezer had decided to revive him; but there had been only money enough to give him operational youth. Not much had been done cosmetically; and it had taken everything he had. 'I bet you've had an interesting life,' Forrester told him solemnly, finishing what remained in his glass.

The man gave him a grave nod. *'Signore,'* he said, *'durante la vita mia prima della morte, era un uomo grande! Nel tempo del Duce – ah! Un maggiore dell esercito, io, e dappertutto non mi dispiacciono le donne!'*

Whitlow patted the old man on the shoulder and led Forrester away. 'Forebrain damage,' he whispered.

'But he was talking in Italian.'

'Sure, Chuck. He can't learn raht, that's what he's doing

here. You know, they ain't many jobs for a fella that can't talk lahk the rest of us.'

The Martian lurched past them, his head twisted sidewise toward them. Whether he had been listening or not Forrester could not say, but he was declaiming, 'Talk like de rest. Live like de rest. Live for de state, for de state knows what's best.'

The whole party was coming to life, thought Forrester, flushed and happy. A small man in a green ruff – it seemed to be an imitation of the Sirian coloration – cried, 'And what's best? Adolf Berle asked it half a millennium ago: "What does a corporation want?" And the state has become a corporation!'

The ballet dancer hiccoughed and opened glazed and angry eyes. 'Stalinist!' she hissed, then returned to sleep; and Forrester dug deep for hundred-dollar bills and fed them to the joymaker slots for more drinks all around.

Forrester was perfectly aware that he was rapidly depleting his last thousand dollars. In a way, it pleased him. He was drunk enough, euphoric enough, to let tomorrow face tomorrow's fears. However badly the next day began, it could not be worse than this one had been. He saw advantages even in being a Forgotten Man: you could spend yourself into pennilessness, but not into bankruptcy; you could never go into debt, since you had no credit to begin with. Wise Tars Tarkas! Excellent kids, to have found him such fine advice. 'Eat!' he cried, shaking off Whitlow's cautionary whisper. 'Drink! Be merry! For tomorrow we die, again!'

'*Domani morire!*' shrilled the old Italian, uptilting his glass of heaven-knows-how-costly grappa that Forrester had provided for him, and Forrester returned the toast.

'Listen, Chuck,' said Whitlow uneasily. 'You better take it slow. We don't get a mark lahk that space fella every day.'

'Whit, shut up. Don't be a grandma, will you?'

'Well, it's your money. But don't blame me if you're broke again tomorrow.'

Forrester smiled and said clearly, 'You make me sick.'

'Now, cut it out raht there!' blazed Whitlow. 'Whur'd you be if it wasn't for me? God damn, Ah don't have to take this kind of—'

But the Martian with the Irish name interrupted them. 'Hey, you fellows! Dat's enough, dere. You got to buy drinks yet.' As Whitlow cooled off, Forrester turned to inspect him; something had been on his mind.

'You,' he said. 'How come you talk like that?'

'Like what, "like dat"? You tink dere's someting funny about de way I talk?'

'Yeah, matter of fact. Why?'

But something had occurred to the Martian. He snapped his fingers. 'Wait a minute! Forrester, is dat what you said your name was?'

'That's right. But we're talking about you—'

'You should learn not to interrupt dat way,' reproved Kevin O'Rourke na Solis Lacis. 'What I want to tell you is dis. Dere's a Sirian been around looking for you.'

'Sirian? One of the green fellows?' Fuzzily Forrester tried to concentrate, but it was not much fun. 'You mean S Four?'

'How de hell would I know his number? He came around in one of dem pressure-cloaks, but I could tell he was a Sirian. I saw plenty of dem.'

'Probably wants to sue me for breach of contract,' Forrester said bitterly. 'He's welcome; there's plenty of others.'

'No, I don't tink so, because—'

'Cut it out,' interrupted Forrester. 'You know, I hate the way you Martians keep changing the subject. What I want to know is why you all talk like that. This other one that wants to kill me, he had the same kraut accent, but in his case it figured, because he had a kraut name. But you talk the same way and you're Irish, right?'

Kevin O'Rourke stared at him disapprovingly. 'Forrester, you're drunk. What de hell's "Irish"?'

How long the party lasted Forrester did not know. He remembered a long harangue in which the drunken ballet

124

ancer was trying to explain to him that the accent was Mar-
an, not German; something to do with six-hundred-
millibar oxyhelium air, which got them out of the habit of
hearing certain frequencies. He had a clear memory of
reaching into his pocket one time and coming up empty; and
a fuzzy, frightening recollection of something bad that had
happened.

But it was all hazy and distant and it came back to him
only in random patches.

What he knew for sure was that when he woke up the next
morning he was back in the rough-hewn tunnel next to the
joymaker shop. How he had gotten there he had no idea.
And he was alone.

Except, that is, for the granddaddy of all hangovers.

He dimly remembered that Whitlow had warned him
about that, too. There were no autonomic monitoring circuits on the public joymakers, Whitlow had said. He would
have to decide for himself when he had had enough, because
the joymaker would not stop service at the point of no
return – not as long as the money held out.

Apparently it had held out too long.

He shook his head miserably. The movement sent cas-
cades of pain down the back of his skull.

Something bad had happened. He tried half-heartedly to
recall it, but all that would come to his memory was a
mosaic of mass terror. *Something* had broken up the party
with drunken men and women racing around in terror, even
the Italian and the ballerina rousing themselves enough to
flee. But what?

He was not sure; and he suspected that he would rather
not remember, not just now.

He lurched to the end of the tunnel, climbed down metal
steps, and pushed a door ajar. He stood gazing out over the
plantings, touched by a warm breeze in which he took no
pleasure at all. It was daylight, and, except for a distant
swish of hovercar traffic, there was no sound of anyone
around.

125

It was too soon to judge, on the basis of less than twenty four hours' experience. And no doubt his troubles were al his own fault. But Forrester was ready to concede that lif with the Forgotten Men was not his place in this new world either.

If he had any place at all.

By the time Whitlow showed up, looking fat and happ and as though hangovers had never existed in the world Forrester had come to the conclusion that, since he wa alive, he would have to go on living.

'Ev'thing all raht this morning?' Whitlow asked cheer fully. 'Man! You were flahing hah when we parted.'

'I'm aware of that,' said Forrester glumly. 'I guess I' have to take your word for the details. Whitlow, how do I g about getting a job again?'

'What for?'

'I think it's time I grew up,' said Forrester abjectly. 'I'n not knocking you. But I don't want to live this way.'

'You better start with some money,' Whitlow offered 'Won't anybody hah'r you if you come in this way.'

'All right. So the first step is to panhandle a stake?'

'Raht!' cried Whitlow. 'And that's whut Ah came to tel you, Chuck! The flah-boy's around again. Whahn't you se if you can score again with him?'

They moved out across the broad green belt under th pylons, looking for open sky. Whitlow had seen the spac pilot in a one-man flier, cruising aimlessly around; accord ing to Whitlow, the man had looked as though he wer about to land and stroll among the Forgotten Men again but there was no sign of him. 'Sorry,' Whitlow apologized 'But Ah'm sure he's around somewhere.'

Forrester shrugged. Truth to tell, he was thinking, h wasn't sure he wanted to panhandle anybody. When yo came right down to it, he had been living off this society without contributing anything in return. Not even anythin in terms of the peculiar values of the society itself; some

126

hing that, it appeared, could be as little as a membership in Taiko's revolutionary society dedicated to its overthrow. With the endless flexibility of employment available, Forester thought, surely there was *something* he could do – something that he would enjoy, and think worth his while to do . . .

'Told you, Chuck!' Whitlow yelled. 'See 'im? There!'

Forrester looked upward, and Whitlow was right. A face looked down from the flier; it looked like the astronaut's face, the eyes regarding them thoughtfully.

The figure picked up a joymaker and whispered into it. The flier dipped and slid away toward a landing.

'He's landing,' said Forrester unnecessarily.

Whitlow was rubbing his chin, watching the flier descend toward the ground. He said abstractedly, 'Uh-huh.' His eyes looked worried.

'What's the matter?' Forrester asked.

'Huh?' Whitlow frowned at him, then back at the flier. 'Oh, nothing, Chuck. Only Ah have a bad feeling raht now.'

'What about?'

'Well . . . Nothing, Chuck. Only you never know what these flah-boys will want to do for fun, an' – Listen, Chuck. Ah believe Ah want to get out of here.' And he turned briskly, catching Forrester's arm to pull him along.

Alarmed only because Whitlow seemed to be alarmed, not yet comprehending what it was all about, Forrester went along. If he thought at all, he only thought that it was rather cowardly of Whitlow to be so fearful, and not untypical of his cowardly age, where the very hope of immortality had produced exaggerated fear of permanent death. It was not until he felt the rush of air overhead that fear struck him personally and acutely.

The flier had taken off again, was now circling over them.

'It's him!' Forrester cried. 'You're right, he is after us!'

He turned and ran, Whitlow dodging away in another direction, the two of them scattering as the flier dipped and turned overhead . . .

127

It was funny, Forrester realized tardily, but he hadn't see the man's face looking out of the flier this time.

At that moment he heard Whitlow's yell. The man hadn' been looking out of the flier. He hadn't even been in it; ha sent the thing on its autonomic circuits into a hovering pat tern, while he himself waited on the ground. And he stoo there now, holding something that looked like a whip directly in Whitlow's path, under the skirt of a taperin yellow building.

Whitlow tried to turn again and run, but he never had chance. The thing that looked like a whip was a whip. Th spaceman seemed only to shake it gently, and its tip hisse out to touch Whitlow, then curled around his neck an threw him to the ground.

Forrester turned and ran. Directly behind him was th hoverway, with its hissing, rocketing, ground-effect cars fol lowing each other like tracer rounds out of a machine gun. I one of them struck him, he would die as surely as at th hands of any assassin; but he did not wait, he flung himsel across the broad strip and miraculously missed them. A copper was standing, regarding him curiously, as Forreste turned to look back.

The spaceman was lifting the whip again, an expression o alert pleasure on his face. Over the *whush* of the hovercar Forrester could hear Whitlow's scream. Their benefacto from space reached out again with the whip as Whitlow trie to rise; he was slashed back to earth again; he tried to get u once more, and his body shook as the whip flicked bloo from the side of his head. He tried again, and was throwi down. And stopped trying.

Forrester turned away and found he was sobbing.

I have a *right* to be scared, he told himself, half crazed. N one could watch a friend whipped to death unmoved. No when the death was so vicious and so pointless. Especiall not when the victim could so easily have been himself.

Could still be himself.

Forrester started to run and blundered into the rudd

metal arms of the copper. 'Man Forrester,' it said, staring into his eyes, 'I have a message for you and good morning.'

'Let go!' shouted Forrester.

'The message is as follows,' said the copper inexorably. 'Man Forrester, will you care to accept reemployment? It is from the one you know as Sirian Four.'

'Let go of me, damn you!' cried Forrester. 'No. Or, yes – I don't know! I just want to get out of here!'

'Your wishful prospective employer, Man Forrester,' said the copper, releasing him, 'is nearby. He will see you now if you wish.'

'He will go plumb to hell,' snarled Forrester, shaking himself. He trotted away, only coincidentally in the direction in which the copper had faced him; but it turned out that no coincidence was involved. The copper had pointed him toward the Sirian's waiting aircar. Forrester saw the aircar first, and outside of it something he did not immediately recognize. It looked a little like a glittering mushroom, a little like a chromium ice cream cone. It rested on ducted jets that swept it across a bed of storm-tossed poppies toward Forrester. It moved toward him very fast, so fast that recognition was tardy; he did not realize it was a pressure suit until he was close enough to see within the bulge of the mushroom, behind an inset band of crystal, a ring of bright green eyes.

It was his Sirian. And it was reaching out to touch him with something that glittered and stung.

Forrester found himself lying on the ground, staring up at the suit that rode beside him on its jets.

'I never said I'd go back to work for you,' he said. It hung there unresponding, the long tendril that had stung him now dangling slackly by its side.

'I don't need a job that bad,' he babbled, squeezing his eyes closed. He thought that whatever the Sirian had stabbed him with was something very peculiar indeed. For he could not move. And the Sirian seemed to be changing shape.

It no longer looked like a Sirian at all.

TWELVE

At some later time Forrester realized that he could move again, and he found that he was in a flier, laughing to himself over something he had forgotten, staring down at a bright golden farm scene below.

A voice from behind him said, 'Dear Charles, you are all right, it is true?'

He turned, grinning. 'Sure. Only I've forgotten some things.'

'You will say what those things are, dear Charles?'

He laughed, 'Oh, what happened to the Sirian. Last I remember, he did something to me – it felt as though he were giving me a hypospray of something. And where we're going – would you believe it, I don't even remember getting into this thing with you. And another thing, I don't remember why you're wearing that funny-looking suit, Adne.'

Adne said nothing, only regarded him roguishly through her circlet of green eyes.

He was no longer laughing. 'It's confusing,' he apologized. 'I'm sorry if I've messed things up again.'

She still did not speak, although she was busy enough. With others of her eyes she was apparently studying the instrument board of the flier, which was marked off in terrain segments, showing their flight plan as they moved.

'Dear Charles,' she said suddenly, 'you are ready to perform your programmed tasks?'

'What programmed tasks?'

But the question was a mistake. An explosion of pain formed under his skull and burst through his body to the tips of fingers and toes, where it recoiled and surged back and forth through his nervous system in dwindling echoes. He cried out. It was not the first time he had felt that pain;

130

he remembered now. And he remembered his programmed tasks.

'You are Adne Bensen. As a joke you want me to smuggle you onto a starship. I must carry you aboard and plug in the command unit you have given me to the starship's circuits and tell no one, or it will spoil the joke. And hurt me.'

'Dear Charles,' boomed the hollow, resonant voice, 'you are ready to perform your programmed tasks.'

The pain was receding. Forrester leaned back, dizzy, sick, extremely confused. He wondered if his mind were breaking down. Certainly it would be no wonder if it were, after what he had been through.

It did not seem to him that Adne's joke was very *funny*. But Forrester recognized that his mind was not very sharp at that moment, and perhaps it was his judgment that was at fault, not the joke. He felt as though he were crazy. He felt both unbearably sleepy and keyed up, like an insomniac glaring hatefully at the slowly brightening window of his room. His eyes were gritty and sore, but when he closed them they sprang open again. It was frightening.

And he was disoriented in space and time. He had no idea where they were. He realized with dismay that it was dark night outside the flier. When had that happened? Time passed that he did not mark in any way; he would look up to see Adne regarding him with her strangely bright green eyes, look again, and she was somewhere else; but he had not seen her move. Delusions. Had he not thought that Adne had stabbed him with something like a hypodermic? What possible motive would she have for that? Had he not seemed to remember her *telling* him who she was over and over? (As though he couldn't recognize her!) Wasn't there a memory of the girl, looking so strangely unlike herself in that Sirian spacesuit, repeating and endlessly repeating instructions on what he was to do at some later time, emphasizing them with jabs of that explosive pain?

He closed his eyes, groaning.

131

They flew open again, but curiously he was not in the flier any more. Dizzy and sick, he saw only in flashes, but the flashes told him that he was standing on hot, baked, dead grass; there was the whir of the flier's idling rotors behind him, ahead of him a metallic whining of gears as a port opened, beside him a hiss of ducted gas. He found himself pushing the bobbing, silent figure in the cone-shaped space-suit through the opening port; found himself connecting something flat and shiny to jacks on an instrument board. And then he was outside again, and under stars, and getting back into the flier.

But where was Adne?

He flung himself petulantly down on the seat. His head was splitting with pain. 'Damn you,' he whispered, and slept.

When he woke up, the flier was standing at the side of the hoverway, across from the tapering yellow spire. The engines were stopped and silent. As best he could tell, it was at the exact spot where the Sirian had reached out for him with the thing that stung.

He staggered out and breathed deep. *Whush* of vehicles from the hoverway, scream of tires from another, more dis-tant road. There was no other sound. It appeared to be morning.

He called tentatively, 'Adne?'

There was no answer. In a way, he had not expected one, only hoped.

Twenty-four hours had disappeared out of his life, and he was very hungry. He searched his pockets, to see what might be left of the handout from his friend, the whip-murderer. Nothing. He had expected that, of course. His resources were dwindling all the time. His money was gone. His credit was destroyed. Whitlow, his mentor among the Forgotten Men, was dead – irrevocably dead, Forrester thought, making the distinction in his mind that this age made out of instinct.

He had only Adne left – if he had Adne. So he did what

he had known all along he was going to do; he headed for Adne's condominium.

He knew perfectly well, as he skulked through the underways and dodged passing fliers, that he had no real claim on her. She might not be home; she might not admit him if she was.

But she was home and did admit him, without much enthusiasm. 'You look a mess,' she said, averting her face. 'All right, come in.'

He sat down, ill at ease. The two children were there, staring with total interest at something on the view-wall. They barely glanced his way, then returned to their show. For that matter, Adne's attention was on the wall as well.

Forrester cleared his throat. He was aware that, besides being hungry and broke, he was also far from clean. He cast about in his mind for some conversational gambit that would give Adne a chance to invite him to eat, or at least to wash up. 'I, uh, had a funny experience,' he said tentatively.

She grunted over her shoulder, 'Hold it, will you, Charles?' She seemed very upset over something, he thought, watching her as she fingered her joymaker and stared at the changing patterns on the view-wall.

He said desperately, 'I thought you were with me yesterday. It was all dreamlike and crazy, and I'm worried. It wasn't you, was it?'

'Charles, will you shut up a minute?' Her attention was on the wall. Forrester glanced at it . . .

And saw a scene that he recognized. It was dried, seared grass on an open plain. There was a mark where something heavy had ground into the earth. A man's voice was saying, in tones of sonorous mourning, 'The liftship appears to have evaded orbital patrols, and so it must be assumed to be on its way to Sirius itself. Radar-net surveillance detected it at launch, and appropriate challenges were issued. But there was no response . . .'

Forrester swallowed a lump in his throat. 'Did – did a Sirian – did one of them escape?'

133

The boy snapped, 'Sweat, Charles! Where've you been? Happened hours ago!'

Forrester let his eyes close on his interior agony. The organ voice of the man narrating from the view-wall continued.

'Meanwhile, there is much concern at every level of authority. There can be no doubt that there must have been human complicity in the escape. Yet no joymaker monitors have registered any such event, nor can any motive be found. The Alliance for Solar-Sirian Amity has voluntarily offered all of its members for mind-probing; eight registered nihilist-obliterative organizations have been questioned about statements of policy suggesting that, in one formulation or another, all of humanity should destroy itself. No information suggesting complicity has emerged.

'But transcending any question of guilt are the considerations of consequence. One fact is beyond argument: a Sirian has managed to begin the long trip back to his home planet, undoubtedly carrying with him the information that Earth is the culprit in the destruction of a Sirian spacecraft. Experts in Sirian psychology declare that the result will be war. All over the world at this hour—'

'He's looping it, Mim,' grumbled the boy. 'We heard this part twice already. Can I shut it off?'

Adne nodded and sank back, her face tense and almost expressionless as the wall relapsed into a decorative jungle scene.

Forrester coughed.

'Oh,' said Adne. 'I almost forgot you were here. Did you want to ask me something?'

'Well,' said Forrester, 'I did, but it isn't important now.'

'Not compared to *this*,' she agreed. 'What was it?'

'Nothing. It was just something about whether you were with me yesterday, but I don't have to ask you anymore. I know who was with me now.'

THIRTEEN

Once, many years before (it was actually several centuries, counting the deep-freeze time), little Chuck Forrester had caused a three-car auto smash that put two people in the hospital.

He had done it with his little slingshot, lying out in the tall grass next to his house in Evanston, taking shots at the cars on the highway. His aim was too good. He hit one. He got a state policeman in the eye. The cop had lost control, jumped into the opposite lane, sideswiped a convertible, and skidded into a station wagon.

Nobody died; the policeman didn't even lose his eye, although it was close for a while; and, as it happened, they didn't think to look around the neighborhood for kids with slingshots. The accident went down on the books as having been caused by a pebble thrown up by a passing car. But Chuck didn't know that, and for a solid year afterward he woke up in a sweat of fear every night, and all his days were horrors of anticipating being caught.

It was just so now.

It was perfectly clear to Forrester that he was the one who had helped the Sirian circumvent the electronic defenses that kept the aliens bound to Earth. He could work it out step by step in his mind. The Sirian had shopped around until it found a human being ignorant enough, and pliable enough, to be unsuspicious. It had contrived to inject him with some hypnotic drug; it had made him believe it was Adne Bensen, then induced him to fly it to the site of an obsolete, but still workable, spaceship – unconscious, or in whatever state in a Sirian passed for unconsciousness, so that the electronic alarms would register nothing. It had commanded him to load it aboard the ship and launch it

135

into space, and he had done as he was commanded, in the fuzzy-minded suggestibility it had doped him into.

Perfectly clear! He could see every step. And, if he could certainly others could. All they had to do was take the trouble to think it through. And certainly all the world was thinking hard about the Sirians. The view-wall was full of news: special investigating teams ransacking the site of the take-off for clues, a hundred new probes launched to guard the perimeter of the solar system. Condition Yellow alert declared, and everyone cautioned to remain within easy distance of a raid shelter at all times.

Forrester kept waiting for the hand to fall on his shoulder and the voice to cry, 'You, Forrester! You are the man!'

But it did not come . . .

Meanwhile, the flap over the escape of Sirian Four had had one good effect, and that was that Adne was so interested in the excitement that she became much more friendly to Forrester again. She even fed him, let him clear himself up in her bath, and, as the children were off on some emergency drill with their age-peers, gave him their room to sleep in when it became obvious he was near collapse.

Voices woke him – Adne's and a man's.

'. . . Mostly for the kids, of course. I'm not so worried for myself.'

'Natch, honey. God! At a time like this! Just when the society's ready to swing.'

'It wouldn't be so bad, but it makes you wonder about a lot of other things. I mean, really, how could they *let* that thing escape?'

A masculine growl: 'Hah! How? Haven't I being telling you how? It's letting machines do men's work! We've put our destiny in the hands of solid-state components, so what do you expect? Don't you remember my White Paper last year! I said, "Guarding men's liberties is a post of honor, and only the honored should hold it." '

Forrester sat up, recognizing the voice: Taiko Hironibi. The Luddite.

'I thought you were talking about the coppers,' said Adne's voice.

'Same thing! Machines should do machine work, men should do men's – Hey, what's that?'

Forrester realized he had made a noise. He stood up, feeling ancient and worn, but somewhat better than before he had slept, and was coming out toward them even before Adne answered Taiko. 'It's only Charles. Come in here, Charles, why don't you?'

Taiko was standing before the view-wall, joymaker in his hand; his thumb was on one of the studs, and apparently he had just been giving himself a shot of one brand or another of euphoria. Even so, he glowered at Forrester.

'Oh, don't be like that,' said Adne.

'Huh,' said Taiko.

'If I can forgive him, you can forgive him. You have to make allowances for the kamikaze ages.'

'Hah,' said Taiko. But the euphoria prevailed – either the spray from the joymaker, or the spice of danger that was sweeping them all. Taiko clipped the joymaker to his belt, rubbed his chin, then grinned, 'Well, why not? All us human beings have to stand together now, right? Put 'er there.'

Gravely they shook hands. Forrester felt altogether ridiculous doing it; he was not sure just what he had done to offend Taiko in the first place, and was not particularly anxious to be forgiven by him now. Still, he reminded himself, Taiko had once offered him a job. A job was something he needed. Although, with the Sirian threat so urgent and imminent now, it was at least an open question whether the Ned Lud Society would need any more workers ...

It could not hurt to find out. Before he could change his mind, Forrester said rapidly, 'I want you to know, Taiko, that I've been thinking a lot about what you said. You were right, of course.'

Taiko's eyes opened. 'About what?'

'About the danger of the machines, I mean. What I think is, men should do men's work and machines should do machine work.'

'Yes?'

'There's only one computer you can trust.' Forrester tapped his skull with a forefinger. 'The one up here.'

'Sure, but—'

'It just burns me up,' said Forrester angrily, 'to think that they left the safeguarding of our planet to solid-state components! If only they'd listened to you!'

With part of his attention, Forrester could hear a smothered giggle from Adne, but he ignored it. 'I want you to know,' he cried, 'that I've come to some conclusions over the last few days and I'm for the Ned Lud Society a hundred percent. Let me help, Taiko! Call on me for anything!'

Taiko gave the girl a look of absent-minded puzzlement, then returned to Forrester. 'Well,' he said, 'I'm glad to hear that. I'll keep that in mind, if anything comes up.'

It took all of Forrester's self-control to keep his expression friendly and eager; why was Taiko being so *slow*? But Adne rescued him. Suppressing her giggles, she said excitedly, 'Say, Taiko! Why don't you let Charles in the Society? I mean, if he'd be willing.'

Taiko frowned and hesitated, but Forrester didn't give him a chance. 'I'm willing,' he said nobly. 'I meant what I said. Glad to help.'

Taiko shrugged after a second and said, 'Well, fine, then, Forrester. Of course, the money's not much.'

'Doesn't matter a bit!' cried Forrester. 'It's what I want to do! Uh, how much?'

'Well, basic scale is twenty-six thousand.'

'A day?'

'Sure, Forrester.'

'It doesn't matter,' said Forrester largely. 'I only want to serve any way I can.' And, exultant, he allowed himself to be given a drink to celebrate, which he enlarged to be a meal. Adne was tolerantly amused.

138

And all the while the view-wall was displaying scenes of alarm and panic, unheeded.

Forrester had not forgotten that he had betrayed Earth to the Sirians; he had only submerged that large and unpleasant thought in the smaller, but more immediate, pleasure of having escaped from the Forgotten Men. He drank a warm, minty froth and ate nutlike little spheres that tasted like crisp pork; he accepted a spray of a pinkly evanescent cloud from Adne's joymaker that made him feel about seventeen again – briefly. Tomorrow would be time enough to worry about what he had done to the world, he thought. For today it was enough to be eating well and to have a place in the scheme of mankind.

But all his worries came back to him when he heard his name spoken. It was Taiko's joymaker that spoke it, and it said, 'Man Hironibi! Permit an interruption, please. Are you in the company of Man Forrester, Charles Dalgleish?'

'Yes, sure,' said Taiko, a beat before Forrester opened his mouth to plead with him to deny it.

'Will you ask Man Forrester to speak his name, Man Hironibi?'

'Go ahead, Forrester. It's to identify you, see?'

Forrester put down the cup of frothed mint and took a deep breath. The pink cloud of joy might as well never have been. He felt every year of his age, even the centuries in the freezer. He said, because he could think of no excuse for not saying it, 'Oh, all right. Charles Dalgleish Forrester. Is that what you want?'

Promptly the joymaker said, 'Thank you, Man Forrester. Your acoustic pattern is confirmed. Will you accept a message of fiscal change?'

That was quick, thought Forrester, clutching at a feeling of relief; the thing only wanted to acknowledge his new job! 'Sure.'

'Man Forrester,' said Taiko's joymaker, 'your late employer, now permanently removed from this ecology, left instructions to disburse his entire residual estate as follows:

to the League for Interspacial Amity, one million dollars; to the Shoggo Central Gilbert and Sullivan Guild, one million dollars; to the United Fraternity of Peace Clubs, five million dollars; the balance, amounting to ninety-one million, seven hundred sixty-three thousand, one hundred forty-two dollars, estimated as of this moment – mark! – to be transferred to the account of his last recorded employee as of date of removal, to wit, yourself. I am now so transferring this sum, Man Forrester. You may draw on it as you wish.'

Forrester sank weakly back against the cushions of Adne's bright, billowy couch. He could not think of anything to say.

'God bless,' cried Adne, 'you're rich again, Charles! Why, you lucky creature!'

'Sure are,' echoed Taiko, grasping his hand warmly. Forrester could only nod.

But he was not really sure that he was so lucky as he seemed. Ninety-one million dollars! It was a lot of money, even in this age of large numbers. It would keep him in comfort for a long time, surely; it would finance all sorts of pleasures and pursuits; it would remove him from the whim of Taiko's pleasure and insure him against a relapse to the Forgotten Men. But what would happen, Forrester thought painfully, when someone asked, first, who that late employer happened to be – and why that employer, before returning to his native planet circling around the star Sirius, had so lavishly rewarded Charles Forrester?

The news from the view-wall kept coming in, in a mounting torrent of apprehension and excitement. Forrester, watching Adne and Taiko as they responded to the news reports, could hardly tell when they were reacting with fear and when with a sense of stimulation. Did they really expect Earth to be destroyed by the retaliation of the Sirians? And what were they going to do about it?

When he tried to ask them, Taiko laughed. 'Get rid of the machines,' he said largely. 'Then we'll take 'em on – any snake or octopus from anywhere in the galaxy! But first we've got to clean house at home.'

Adne only said, 'Why don't you come with us – and relax?'

'Relax how?'

'Come along and see,' she said.

Considering his own guilt in that area, Forrester did not want to attract attention by seeming *specially* concerned about the Sirians. But he insisted, 'Shouldn't somebody be doing something?'

'Somebody will be,' said Taiko. 'Don't worry so, boy! There'll be a run on the freezers – people chickening out, you see. You know. "Leave it to George." Then, by and by, the Sirians'll come nosing around, and the appropriate people will deal with them. Or they won't.'

'Meanwhile, Taiko and I have a date to crawl,' said Adne, 'and you might as well come along. It'll rest you.'

'Crawl?'

'It's everybody's duty to keep fit – now more than ever,' Taiko urged.

'You're being very good to me,' Forrester said gratefully. But what he really wanted was to sit in that room and watch the view-wall. One by one the remote monitoring stations of Earth's defense screen were reporting in, and although the report from each one of them so far was the same – 'No sign of the escaped Sirian' – Forrester wanted to stay with it, stay right in that room watching that view-wall, until there was some other report. To make sure that Earth was safe, of course. But also to find out, at the earliest possible moment, if the (hopefully) recaptured Sirian would give out any information about his accomplice . . .

'Well, we're going crawling,' said Adne. 'And we really ought to take off right now.'

Forrester said irritably, 'Wait a minute. What did they just say about Groombridge 1830?'

'They said what they've been saying for a week, *dear*

Charles. That thing they spotted is only a comet. Are we going to crawl or aren't we?'

Taiko said humorously, 'Charles is still a little dazed about his new loot. But look, old buddy, some of us have got things to do.'

Forrester took his eyes from the view-wall's star map and looked at Taiko, who winked and added, 'Now that you're on the team, you ought to learn the ropes.'

'Team?' said Forrester. 'Ropes?'

'I have to do a communication for the society,' Taiko explained. 'You know. What you used to call a widecast. And as you're on the payroll now you ought to come along and see how it's done, because frankly—' he nudged Charles— 'It won't be too long before you're doing them yourself.'

'But first we crawl,' said Adne. 'So shall we the sweat get *going*?'

They hustled Forrester along, muttering and abstracted as he was, until he realized that he was attracting attention to himself, and he didn't want to do *that*.

It might be, thought Forrester, that the right and proper thing for him to do was to go to someone in authority – if he ever found anyone in authority in this world, except maybe the joymaker – and say, frankly and openly, 'Look, sir. I seem to have done something wrong and I wish to make a statement about it. Under what I guess was hypnosis I made it possible for that Sirian to escape, thus blowing the whole security of the human race forever.' Confess the whole thing and take his medicine.

Yes, he thought, some time I probably had better do just that; but not right now.

Meanwhile, he tried to look as much like everybody else as he possibly could, and if this required him to be thrilled but casual about the danger of an invasion fleet of Sirians appearing in the sky at any moment to crush the Earth, then he would do his best to seem thrilled but casual.

'Well,' he cried gaily, 'we sure had a good run for our

142

money! Best little old masters of the planet *I* ever saw! But may the best race win, right?'

Adne looked at him, then at Taiko, who shrugged and said, 'I guess he's still a little shook.'

Dampened, Forrester concentrated on observing what was going on around him. Taiko and the girl were bringing him to a part of Shoggo he had not previously visited, south along the shore to what looked like a leftover World's Fair. Their cab landed and let them out in a midway, bustling with groups and couples in holiday mood, surrounded by buildings with a queer playtime flavor. Nor was the flavor confined to the buildings. The place was a carnival of joy and of what Forrester at once recognized as concupiscence. The aphrodisiac spray that individual joymakers dispensed in microgram jolts was here a mist hanging in the air. The booths and displays were shocking to Forrester, at first, until he had taken a few deep breaths of the tonic, the invigorating air. Then he began at last to enjoy himself.

'That's better,' cried Adne, patting him. 'Down this way, past the Joy Machine!'

Forrester followed along, observing his surroundings with increasing relaxation and pleasure. In addition to its other attractions, the place was a horticultural triumph. Flowers and grasses grew out of the ground he walked on and along the margins at his sides; out of elevated beds that leaned out to the midway, heavy with emerald grapes and bright red luminous berries; out of geometrical plantings that hung on the sides of the buildings. Even on the walk itself, among the happy humans, there were what looked like shrubs bearing clusters of peach- and orange-colored fruits – but they moved, walked, stumped clumsily and slowly about on rootlike legs.

'In here,' said Adne, clutching at his arm.

'Hurry up!' cried Taiko, shoving him.

They entered a building like a fort and went down a ramp surrounded by twinkling patterns of light. The concentration of joymaker spray was a dozen times stronger here than in the open air. Forrester, feeling lightheaded, began to look at Adne with more interest than he would have believed himself able to show in anything but Sirians. Adne leaned close to nibble his ear; Taiko laughed in pleasure. They were not alone, for there was a steady stream of people going down the ramp with them, fore and aft, all with flushed faces and excited.

Forrester abandoned himself to the holiday. 'After all,' he shouted to Adne, 'what does it matter if we're going to be wiped out?'

'Dear Charles,' she answered, 'shut up and take your clothes off.'

Surprised, but not very, Forrester saw that the whole procession was beginning to shed its outer garments. Shaggy vests and film-and-net briefs, they were tossed on the floor, where busy glittering little cleaning creatures tugged them away into disposal units. 'Why not?' he laughed, and kicked his slipper at one of the cleaners, which reared back on its wheels like a kitten and caught it in midair. The crowd rolled down the ramp, shedding clothes at every step, until they were in a sort of high-vaulted lounge and the noise of laughter and talk was loud as a lynching.

And then a door behind them closed. The cloying joy-maker scent whisked away. Streams of a harsher, colder essence poured in upon them; and at once they were all standing there, nearly nude and cold sober.

Charles Forrester had had something less than four decades of actual life – that is to say, of elapsed time measured by lungs that breathed and a heart that beat. The first part of that life, measured in decades, had taken place in the twentieth century. The second part, measured in days, had taken place after more than half a millennium in the freezing tanks.

Although those centuries had sped by tracelessly for Forrester, they represented real time to the world of men: each century a hundred years, every year 365 days of twenty-four hours each.

Of all that had happened during those centuries, Forrester had managed to learn only the smallest smattering. He had not learned, even yet, what powers this century could pack into a wisp of gas. Playing with the studs of his joymaker or submitting to the whims of his friends, Forrester had tasted a variety of intoxicants and euphorics, wake-up jolts and sleepy jolts. But he had never before tasted the jolt that drugged no senses but sharpened them all. Now he stood in this room, Taiko on one side of him and Adne in the circle of his arm, surrounded by half a hundred other men and women; and he was fully awake and *sensing* for the first time in his life.

He turned to look at Adne. Her face was scrubbed bare, her eyes were looking at him unwinkingly. 'You're nasty inside,' she said.

What she said was the exact equivalent of a slap in the face, and Forrester accepted it as such. A cleansing anger filled his mind. He growled, 'You're a trollop. I think your children are illegitimate, too.' He had not intended to say anything of the sort.

Taiko said, 'Shut up and crawl.'

Over his shoulder and without passion, Forrester said, 'You're a two-bit phony without an ounce of principle or a thought in your head. Butt out, will you?'

To his surprise, Adne was nodding in agreement; but she said, 'Pure kamikaze, just like the trash you come from. Vulgar and a fool.' He hesitated, and she said impatiently, 'Come on, kamikaze. Let it out. You're jealous too, right?'

Theirs was not the only argument going on; there was a bitter rumble of insult and vituperation all around them. Forrester was only marginally aware of it; his whole attention was concentrated on Adne, on the girl he had thought he might be in love with, and his best efforts were devoted to trying to hurt her. He snapped, 'I bet you're not even pregnant!'

She looked startled. 'What?'

'All that talk about picking a name! You probably just wanted to trick me into marrying you.'

She stared at him blankly, then with revulsion. 'Sweat! I meant our *reciprocal* name. Charles, you talk like an idiot.'

Taiko shrilled, 'You're both idiots! *Crawl.*'

Forrester spared him a glance. Curiously, Taiko was down on his knees and for the first time Forrester realized that the floor was damp – not damp, muddy. A thin gruel of softly oozing mud was pouring in from apertures in the wall. Others were getting down into the mud, too; and, for possibly the thousandth time since being taken from the freezer, Forrester found himself torn between two choices of puzzles to try to solve. What was going on here, exactly? And what the devil did Adne mean by 'our' name?

But she tugged at him impatiently, slipping down to wallow in the porridgy substance. 'Come on,' she cried. 'You're not doing it right, but come on, you sweaty kamikaze.'

All the while the air was being recharged with the stimulant, if it was a stimulant, that had opened the gates of his senses for Forrester. It was like LSD, he thought, or a super-Benzedrine: he was seeing a whole new spectrum; hearing bat shrieks and subsonic roars; smelling, tasting, feeling things that had been out of his reach before. He perceived clearly that this was some sort of organized ritual he was in, understood that its purpose was to allow the release of tensions by saying whatever the inner mind had wanted to say and the outer censor in the brain had forbidden. Allow it? He could not stop it! He listened to the things he was saying to Adne and realized that, at a later time, in an undrugged moment, he would be appalled. But he said them.

And she nodded gravely and replied in kind. 'Jealous!' she shrieked. 'Typical manipulative ownership! Filthy inside, trashy!'

'Why shouldn't I be jealous? I *loved* you.'

'Harem love!' sneered Taiko from beside him. The man was lying full length in the mud now – it had reached a depth of several inches and seemed to have stopped there. 'She's a brainless blot of passions, but she's human, and how *dare* you try to own her?'

'Fake!' howled Forrester. 'Go pretend you're a man! Bust up some machines!' He was furious, but in one part of his mind he was alert enough and analytical enough to be surprised that he wasn't impelled to hit Taiko. Or Adne, for that matter. What he was impelled to do was to say wounding things, as true and hurtful as he could make them. He looked around him and saw that he was the only one still on his feet. The others were all full-length in the mud, writhing and creeping. Forrester dropped to his knees. 'What's this damn foolishness all about?' he demanded.

'Shut up and crawl,' grunted Taiko. 'Get some of the animal out of you.' And Adne chimed in, 'You're spoiling it for all of us if you don't crawl! You have to crawl before you can walk.'

Forrester leaned down to her. 'I don't *want* to crawl!'

'Have to. Helps you get out the rot. The secrets that fester ... Of course, you kamikazes like to decay.'

'But I don't have—'

And Forrester paused, not because he had voluntarily chosen to stop talking just then, but because what he had been about to say was not true, and he simply could not say it. He had been about to say that he had no secrets.

He had, in fact, more secrets than he could count; and one very large one that appalled him, because his mouth wanted to blurt it out even while his brain screamed *No!*

If he stayed in this room one more moment, Forrester knew, he would shout at the top of his voice the fact that he had been the one to help the Sirian escape and thus had made it a good gambling bet that the whole world of men would be destroyed. Dripping mud, panting, mumbling to himself, Forrester climbed to his feet and forced himself to run – a staggering, broken-field run that dodged flailing limbs and leaped over writhing bodies, that carried him through the angry rumble of the crawlers and out into a

147

dressing chamber, where he was sluiced down with fragrant spray, dried with warm blasts of air, and bathed in hot light. Fresh garments appeared before him, but he took no pleasure in them. He had forgotten for a moment, but now he remembered again.

He was the man who had destroyed Earth. At any moment he would be found out ... And what his punishment might be, he dared not think.

'Man Forrester,' cried the voice of a joymaker, 'during the period of interrupted service, a number of messages accumulated for you, of which the following three priority calls are urgent.'

'Wait up,' said Forrester, startled. But there it was. Rummaging through the neatly folded heap of T-shirt and Turkish pants, he came upon the macelike shape of a joymaker. 'Ho,' he said, 'I've got you again, eh?'

'Yes, Man Forrester,' the joymaker agreed. 'Will you receive your messages?'

'Um,' said Forrester. Then, cautiously, 'Well, I will if any of them are of great urgency at this very moment. I mean, I don't want somebody coming in here and blowing my brains out while I'm talking to you.'

'No such probability is evident,' said the joymaker primly. 'Nevertheless, Man Forrester, there are a number of highly important messages.'

Forrester sat down on a warmed bench and sighed. He said meditatively, 'The thing is this, joymaker. I never seem to get to the end of a question, because two new questions pop up while I'm still trying to find the answer to the first one. So what I would like to do right now, I would like you to get me a cup of black coffee and a pack of cigarettes, right here in this nice, warm, safe room, and then I would like to drink the coffee and smoke a cigarette and ask you some questions. Now, can I do that without dying for it?'

'Yes, Man Forrester. However, it will take several minutes for the coffee and cigarettes to be delivered, as they

148

are not stock items in this facility and must be secured from remote inventories.'

'I understand all that. Just get them. Now.' Forrester stood up and drew the baggy pants over his legs, thinking. At last he nodded to himself.

'First question,' he said. 'I just came out of a place where Adne Bensen and a bunch of other people were wallowing in mud. What was that all about? – I mean,' he added hastily, 'in a few words, what is it called, and why do people do it?'

'The function is called a "crawl session," Man Forrester, or simply "crawling." Its purpose is the release of tensions and inhibitions for therapeutic purposes. Two major therapies are employed. First, there is a chemical additive in the air that suppresses inhibitors of all varieties, thus making it possible to articulate, and thus to relieve, many kinds of tensions. Second, the mere act of learning to crawl all over again is thought to provide benefits. I have on immediate access, Man Forrester, some thirty-eight papers on various aspects of the crawl session. Would you care to have me list them?'

'Not in the least,' said Forrester. 'That's fine; I understand that perfectly. Now, second question.'

There was a *thunk*; a receptacle opened beside him; Forrester reached in and took out a steaming and very large cup of coffee covered with a plastic lid. He worried the lid off, sought and found the cigarettes and lighter that accompanied the coffee, lit up, took a sip of the coffee, and said, 'Adne Bensen said something to me about choosing a name. I interpreted this to mean that she was, ah, well, pregnant. I mean, I thought she meant a name for a baby; but actually it was something else. Reciprocal names? What are reciprocal names?'

'Reciprocal names, Man Forrester,' lectured the joymaker, 'are chosen, usually by two individuals, less typically by larger groups, as private designations. A comparable institution from your original time, Man Forrester, might be the "pet" name or nickname by which a person addressed his

149

or her spouse, child, or close friend; however, the reciprocal name is used by each of the persons in addressing the other.'

'Give me a for instance,' Forrester interrupted.

'For instance,' said the joymaker obediently, 'in the universe of Adne Bensen and her two children, the reciprocal names are "Tunt" – a form of address from one child to the other – or "Mim", when Miss Bensen addresses or is addressed by a child. As mentioned, this situation is not typical, since more than two persons are involved. A better example from the same demesne would be the relationship of Adne Bensen and Dr Hara, where the reciprocal designation between them is "Tip". Are those adequate for instances, Man Forrester?'

'Yeah, but what's this about Hara? You mean he and Adne have a pet name?'

'Yes, Man Forrester.'

'Yeah, but – Well, skip it.' Forrester glumly put down his coffee; it didn't taste as good as he had thought it would. 'Sounds confusing,' he muttered.

'Confusing, Man Forrester?'

'Yeah. I mean, if you and I have the same name, how do we know which one – Oh, wait a minute. I see. If you and I have a name, then if *you* use it, obviously you mean me. And if I use it, I have to mean you.'

'That is correct, Man Forrester. In practice it does not appear that much confusion arises.'

'All right, the hell with that, too. Let's see.' Forrester frowned at his cigarette; it didn't taste particularly good, either. He was unable to decide whether the reason was that he had lost the taste for coffee and cigarettes, or whether these were simply miserable examples of their kind, or whether what tasted bad was his mood. He dropped the cigarette into the rest of the coffee and said irritably, 'Question three. Now that I have you again, and plenty of money, is there some way I can keep from foolishly losing it all again? Can we like work out a budget?'

'Certainly, Man Forrester. One moment. Yes. Thank you

for waiting. I have obtained a preliminary investment schedule and prospectus of probable returns. By investing a major fraction of your holdings in the Sea of Soup, with diversification in power, computation, and euphoric utilities, you should have a firm annual income in excess of eleven million, four hundred thousand dollars. This can be prorated by week or by day, if you wish, and automatic limits placed on the amounts you can spend or hypothecate. In this way it will be possible – *Man Forrester!*'

Forrester was startled. 'What the devil's the matter with you?'

'Your instructions, Man Forrester! Urgent priority override: statement made earlier that you are in no immediate danger of death is no longer true. Man Heinzlichen Jura de Syrtis Major, having filed appropriate bonds and guaranties—'

'Oh, no!' cried Forrester. 'Not that crazy Martian again!'

'Yes, Man Forrester! Coming through the crawl chamber right now, armed, armored, and looking for you!'

FOURTEEN

Forrester snapped tight the baggy trousers, tucked in the pullover, slipped his feet into sandals, and hooked the joymaker to his belt. 'Out!' he barked. 'Which way?'

'This way, Man Forrester.' An opening in the wall widened like a pair of parentheses, and Forrester bolted through it. A lounge, a ramp, an open double door, and he was out into the midway again, with the bright sun pounding down on him, the gay crowds staring at him casually.

He glanced around: yes, there was the DR vehicle, shining white overhead, its attendant with chin on hand gazing into space. 'Where's Heinzie?' he cried.

'Following, Man Forrester. Do you wish to fight him here?'

'Hell, no!'

'Where would you prefer, Man Forrester?'

'You idiot, I don't want to fight him at all. I want to get away from him.'

He was attracting attention from the crowd, he saw. Their expressions were no longer vacant, but puzzled, and beginning to be hostile.

The joymaker said hesitantly, 'Man Forrester, I must ask you to be specific. Do you wish to avoid combat with Man Heinzlichen *permanently*?'

'That's the idea,' Forrester said bitterly. 'But I see it's a little late for that now.' Because the Martian was churning out of the double doors of the crawling building and heading straight for him. 'Oh, well,' said Forrester. 'Easy come, easy go.'

The Martian planted himself in front of Forrester, puffing. He said, 'Hello, dere. Sorry I kept you waiting so long.'

'You didn't have to hurry on my account,' said Forrester cautiously. He was scanning the Martian carefully for weapons, but there didn't seem to be anything. He was wearing what looked like a wig, close blond curls that hugged his scalp, surrounded his ears and jawline, and went down in back to the nape of his neck, but otherwise he was unchanged in appearance from the last time Forrester had seen him. And he did not even carry a stick. His joymaker was clipped to his belt; his hands were empty and hung loosely at his sides.

'Vell,' said the Martian, 'you were with de Forgotten Men, you know, and den I had other things to do. Anyway, here we are, so let's get it over with. O.K.?'

Forrester said honestly, 'I don't know what I'm supposed to do.'

'Fight, you fool!' cried the Martian. 'What de hell do you think you're supposed to do?'

'But I'm not even mad,' Forrester objected.

'Dog sweat!' roared the Martian. 'I am! Come on, fight, will you?' But his hands still hung at his sides.

Forrester shifted position cautiously, sparing the time for a glance around. The crowd was definitely interested now, forming a neat ring around them; Forrester thought he could see bets being made on the outcome. The DR man overhead was watching them carefully. At least, Forrester thought, if I let him kill me, they'll just freeze me up again. And then they'll put me back together later on. And maybe the freezer isn't such a bad place to be for a while, until this business with the Sirians gets straightened out . . .

'Are you going to fight or not?' the Martian demanded.

Forrester said, 'Uh, one question.'

'Vell?'

'The way you talk. I had an argument about that the other day—'

'What's de matter with de way I talk?'

'It's a sort of German accent, I thought, but this other Martian was Irish, and he talked the same way—'

153

'Irish? German?' Heinzlichen looked baffled. 'Look, Forrester, on Mars we got six-hundred-millibar pressure, you understand? You lose some of de high frequencies, dat's all I don't know what "German" or "Irish" is.'

'Say, that's interesting!' Forrester cried. 'You mean it's not an accent, really?'

'I mean you wasted too much of my time already!' the Martian cried and leaped for his throat. And right there, in the bright midway with the ambulatory plants jolting past him and the crowds cheering and shouting, Forrester found himself fighting for his life. The Martian was not only bigger than he was, the damned skunk was stronger! Fleetingly Forrester blazed with anger: how dare the Martian be stronger? What about the supposition that light-gravity inhabitants would lose their muscle tone? Why was he not able to crush this flimsy, light-G creature with a single blow?

But he could not; the Martian was on top of him, systematically thudding his head against the paving of the midway. It was Forrester's good fortune that the flooring was a resilient, rubber-like substance, not concrete; all the same, he was developing a headache, and his senses were spinning. And now the Martian added insult to injury. 'Get up and fight!' he bawled. 'Dis is no fun!'

That marked the limit of Forrester's civilized control. He screamed in rage and surged up; the Martian went flying. Forrester was up and after him, flinging himself on top of him, a knee in the Martian's throat; he saw the Martian's joymaker loose by his side and caught it up – grabbed it like a club, smashed the macelike large end against the Martian's skull. It rang like bronze. Even in his rage Forrester felt a moment's astonishment; but clearly the close-cropped blond wig was not merely hair, it was a protective armor skullpiece. 'Louse!' roared Forrester, enraged all over again; the Martian had prepared himself for this battle by wearing a helmet! He shortened his stroke and clubbed the Martian across the face. Blood spurted, teeth broke. Again and

154

again, and the Martian tried to cry out but could not; again, again—

Behind him the voice of the attendant from the DR cart said, 'All right, all right, that's enough. I'll take care of him now.'

Forrester rocked back on his haunches, panting hoarsely, staring at the terrible ruin he had made of the Martian's face. He managed to gasp, 'Is – is he dead?'

'They don't come any deader,' said the DR man. 'Would you move a little bit? – Thanks. All right, he's mine now. Wait here for the copper, please; he'll take care of filling out a report.'

What happened next for Forrester was hazy. He had a confused memory of returning to the lavatory facilities of the crawl room and getting cleaned up again, a shower, fresh clothes, a steam of reviving gases that woke him up and cleared his head. But when he was out of the room the fog returned; it was not the drain resulting from his efforts that muddled his thinking, or the aching pain in his head where Heinzie had bashed it against the pavement. It was pure psychic shock.

He had destroyed a human life.

Not really, he told himself at once. Not now. A short rest in the freezer and then he's good as new!

But it didn't register with him; he was still in shock – and puzzled. He could not decide: had he imagined it, or had the Martian not been fighting back?

Adne was waiting for him, with Taiko; they had seen the fight and had stayed to help him get straightened out afterward. Help him or help the Martian, Forrester thought bitterly. It probably didn't matter to them which. Nevertheless, he was grateful for their help. Adne took him to her own home, left him there a minute, returned with the news that his apartment was ready for him again, and escorted him there. And left him with Taiko, who wanted to talk. 'Nice fight, Charles. Shook you up, of course – hell, I remember

155

my own first killing. Nothing to be ashamed of. But, listen, if you're going to come to work for the society you've got to pull yourself together.'

Forrester sat up and looked at Taiko. 'What the devil makes you think I want to work for the Luddites?'

'Come on, Charles. Look, take a shot of bracer, will you? That green stud, there on the handle—'

'Will you get out of here and leave me alone?'

'Oh, for sweat's sake,' cried Taiko impatiently. 'Look, you said you wanted to help out with the society's program, right? Well, there's no time to waste! This is the chance we've been waiting for, man! Everybody's got the Sirians on their minds; they'll be diving into the freezers so fast the teams won't be able to handle them, and that's when those of us who can face the world realistically will have a chance to take action. We can get rid of the machine menace once and for all if we—' Taiko hesitated and gave Forrester a thoughtful look. Then he said, 'Well, never mind that part of it just yet. Are you with us or against us?'

Forrester contemplated the problem of trying to explain to Taiko that his interest in the Ned Lud Society had been only an interest in making enough money to live on, and that, when the Sirian had left him ninety-three million dollars, that interest had evaporated. It did not seem worth the effort, so he said, 'I guess I'm against you.'

'Charles,' said Taiko, 'you make me sick! You of all people! You, who have suffered so much from this age. Don't you want to try to cure the evils of machine domination? Don't you want—'

'I'll tell you what I want,' said Forrester, rousing himself. 'I want you to go away – fast!'

'You're not yourself,' said Taiko. 'Look, when you get straightened out, give me a call. I'll be hard to reach, because – Well, never mind why. But I'll leave a special channel for you. Because I know you, Charles, and I know that you'll have to decide you want to end these cowardly times and give man back his – All right! I'm going!'

When the door had closed behind him, Forrester stared into space for more than an hour. Then he rolled over and went to sleep. His only regret was that sooner or later he would wake up.

FIFTEEN

What Forrester could not understand was why it was taking them so long to arrest him.

He began to see just why a criminal might give himself up. The waiting was hard to endure. Ten times an hour he reached for the joymaker to say, 'I am the one who helped the Sirian escape. Report me to the police,' and ten times each hour he stopped himself. Not now, he said. Tomorrow no doubt, or maybe even a few minutes from now; but not just now.

From time to time the joymaker informed him of messages – forty-five of them the first day alone. Forrester refused to accept them all. He didn't want to see anyone until – until – Well, he didn't want to see anyone at the moment. (He could not make up his mind at just what moment the world would so clarify itself to him that he would be willing to start living in it again; but he always knew that that time was certainly not yet.) He explored the resources of his apartment, the joymaker, and his own mind. He ate fantastic meals and drank odd foaming beverages that tasted like stale beer or celery-flavored malted milks. He listened to music and watched canned plays. He wished desperately for a deck of cards, but the joymaker did not seem to understand his description of them, and so solitaire was denied him; but he found almost the same anesthesia in reading and reading over again what scraps of written matter he had on hand. His late wife's letter he practically memorized; his briefing manual for this century he studied until his fingers were weary from turning the pages.

On the second day there were nearly seventy messages. Forrester refused them all.

At his direction the joymaker displayed for him selected

ews pictures on the view-wall. The only subject Forrester would allow himself an interest in was the progress of the trouble with the Sirians. There was strangely little news after the first day – negative reports from drone patrols in every quadrant of the heavens, a diminishing flow of projections and estimates as to when an attack might be expected. The consensus seemed to be: not for several weeks at least. Forrester could not understand that at all. He remembered quite distinctly that Sirius was something like fifty light-years away, and the joymaker confirmed that no way had been found to exceed the speed of light. Finally he gathered that the Sirians were thought to have some sort of faster-than-light message capability, as did Earth for that matter; so that, even if the fleeing Sirian did not make it back to his own planet, he might send a message. And it was a possibility, at least, that some wandering Sirian war patrol might be near Sol.

But none made itself evident; and on the third day there were only a dozen messages for Forrester; and he refused them all.

What he did with most of his time was sleep.

He had ninety-three million dollars and perfect health. He could think of no better way to spend either of them.

'Joymaker! Tell me what I did wrong with Adne.'

'Wrong in what sense, Man Forrester? I have no record of antisocial acts.'

'Don't split hairs with me. I mean, why didn't she like me after the first few days?'

The joymaker began to answer with statements about hormone balances, imprinting, and the ineluctable components of emotions, but Forrester was having none of it. Get me a beer,' he ordered, 'and give me specific answers. You hear everything that happens, right?'

'Right, Man Forrester. Except when instructed otherwise.'

'All right. I offended her. How?'

159

'I cannot evaluate the magnitude of the offenses, Man Forrester, but I can list certain acts that would appear to be of greater significance than others. Item, you refused her offer of a reciprocal name.'

'That was bad?'

'It is offensive by social convention, Man Forrester, yes.'

The glass of beer appeared by Forrester's couch; he tasted it and made a face.

'No, not that,' he said. 'What was that other thing, the beer with some kind of raspberry sauce?'

'*Berlinerweisse*, Man Forrester?'

'Yeah, get me one of those. Go on with the list.'

'Item, your actions when Man Heinzlichen Jura de Syrtis Major filed intent to kill you were considered contemptible in certain lights.'

'Didn't she understand that I wasn't used to the way things go now?'

'Yes, Man Forrester, she did. Nevertheless, she considered your behavior contemptible. Item, you allowed yourself to become impoverished. Item, you criticized her for a relationship with other males.'

The large goblet of pale beer appeared along with a little flask of dark red syrup; Forrester decanted the syrup into the beer and sipped it. It too tasted terrible, but he had run out of things to ask for and he drank it. 'It was only that I loved her,' he said irritably.

'There are ineluctable aspects to the syndrome "love" which we cannot distinguish, Man Forrester.'

'Hell, I don't expect you to. You're a machine. But I thought Adne was a woman.'

'I can only surmise from the evidence of her responses that she did not comprehend or accept your behavior either, Man Forrester.'

'I have to admit you've got a point there,' sighed Forrester, putting down the goblet and getting up to roam around. 'Well, never mind.' He rubbed his chin thoughtfully, then waved a hand; a mirror appeared, and he studied his face in it. He looked like a bum. Hair unkempt, beard beginning to grow again. 'Oh, hell,' he said.

The joymaker made no answer.

What Forrester really wanted to know – whether anyone had come to suspect him of being the one who had let the Sirian escape – he dared not ask. The questions he did ask, on the other hand, turned out to have answers as confusing as the questions were. Even simple questions. He had asked after his friend among the Forgotten Men, Jerry Whitlow, for example. He had not been surprised to find out that Whitlow was dead – he had seen that happen; or to learn that his revival was problematical; but he still did not know what the joymaker meant by saying that Whitlow was 'returned to reserve.' It *seemed* to mean that Whitlow's body had been used as raw material, perhaps in one of the organic lakes like the 'Sea of Soup,' from which the world's food supplies came; but Forrester was too repelled by that notion to follow it any further, and even so he could not understand why Whitlow's revival would then be 'problematical.'

'How many messages today, joymaker?' he asked idly.

'There are no messages for you today, Man Forrester.'

Forrester turned to look at the thing. That was a welcome surprise – any change was welcome – but it was worrisome, too. Had everyone forgotten him?

'No messages?'

'None that you have not already refused, Man Forrester.'

'Doesn't anyone want to talk to me?'

'As far as indicated by the message log, Man Forrester, only Man Hironibi wishes to talk to you. He left special instructions in regard to forwarding of communications. But that was six days ago.'

Forrester was startled. 'How the devil long have I been here?'

'Nineteen days, Man Forrester.'

He took a deep breath.

Nineteen days! How little his so-called friends cared for

him! he told himself with self-pity. If they *really* liked him they would have broken the door down, if necessary.

But it was not all bad. Nineteen days? But surely, if he were going to be arrested for helping the Sirian escape, it would not have taken this long. Was it safe to assume the heat was off? Did he dare go back into the world of men?

He made up his mind rapidly and, before he could change it, acted at once. 'Joymaker! Get me cleaned up. Shave, bath, new clothes. I'm going outside!'

His resolve lasted him through the cleaning-up process and into the condominium hall, but then it began to dissipate.

No one was in the hall; there were no sounds. But to Forrester it seemed like a jungle trail with unknown dangers on every side. He ordered an elevator cab to take him to slideway level, and when the door opened he entered it cautiously, as though an enemy might be lurking inside.

But it too was empty. And so – he found a moment later – was the wide hoverway. There was simply nothing there.

Forrester stared around, unable to believe what he saw. No pedestrians – well, that was understandable. There were seldom very many, and he had no idea what time of day it was. No hovercraft? That was harder to accept. Even if for a moment none were in sight, he should be able to hear the hissing roar of their passage somewhere in the city. But to see no aircraft, no sign of life at all – that was flatly unbelievable.

Where was everybody?

He said, with a quaver in his voice, 'Get me a cab.'

'One will arrive in two minutes, Man Forrester.' And it did – a standard automated aircab; and Forrester still had not seen a human being. He climbed in quickly, closed the door, and ordered it to take him up – not up to any place in particular, just up, so that he could see farther in all directions.

But no matter how far he looked, no one was there.

162

Words forced themselves out. 'Joymaker! What's happened?'

'In what respect, Man Forrester?' the machine benignly asked.

'Where did everybody go? Adne? The kids?'

'Adne Bensen and her children, Man Forrester, at present are being processed for storage in Sublake Emergency Facility Nine. However, it is not as yet known whether space will be available for them there on a permanent basis, and so the location must be considered tentative pending the completion of additional facilities—'

'You mean they're *dead*?'

'Clinically dead, Man Forrester. Yes.'

'How about—' Forrester cast about in his mind – 'let's see, that Martian. Not Heinzie, the one with the Irish name, Kevin O'Rourke; is he dead, too?'

'Yes, Man Forrester.'

'And the Italian ballerina I met at the restaurant where the Forgotten Men hung out?'

'Also dead, Man Forrester.'

'What the hell *happened*?' he shouted.

The joymaker replied carefully, 'Speaking objectively, Man Forrester, there has been an unforecast increase in the number of commitments to freezing facilities. More than ninety-eight point one percent of the human race is now in cryogenic storage. In subjective terms, the causes are not well established but appear to relate to the probability of invasion by extra-Solarian living creatures, probably Sirian.'

'You mean everybody committed suicide?'

'No, Man Forrester. Many preferred to be killed by others; for example, Man Heinzlichen Jura de Syrtis Major. He, you will recall, elected to be killed by you."

Forrester sank back against the seat. 'Holy sweet heaven,' he muttered to himself. Dead! Nearly the whole human race, dead! It was more than he could take in at once. He sat staring into space until the joymaker said apologetically, 'Man Forrester, do you wish to select a destination?'

'No – wait a minute, yes! Maybe I do. You said ninety-eight percent of the human race is dead.'

'Ninety-eight point one, yes, Man Forrester.'

'But that means there are some who are still alive, right? Are there any I know?'

'Yes, Man Forrester. Certain classes are still in vital state in large proportion because of special requests made for their services – e.g. medical specialists working in the freezer stations. Also, there are others. One you know is Man Hiro-nibi. He is not only in vital state but has, as you know, given special instructions in regard to receiving messages from you.'

'Fine!' cried Forrester. 'Just take me to Taiko, right away! I want to see someone who's alive!'

Because – went the unspoken corollary – he didn't want to see the ruins left by the dead. Not as long as he was so completely convinced that it was he himself who had killed them.

SIXTEEN

But, as it turned out, the cab did not take him to see Taiko after all.

It did what it could. The joymaker programmed it properly enough, and Forrester found himself high in a building of bright ruby crystal, in front of a door inscribed THE NED LUD SOCIETY. Inside was what he supposed was the latter-day equivalent of an office – although it was warm and damp and a fountain played among ferns. But no one was inside.

'What the devil's the matter with you, joymaker?' he demanded. 'Where's Taiko?'

'Man Forrester,' said the joymaker, 'there is an anomaly here. My records indicate Man Hironibi's presence at this place, but clearly they are wrong. My records have never been wrong before.'

'Well, let me talk to him. You said he'd left special instructions about that.'

'Yes, Man Forrester.' Pause. Then Taiko's voice came on. 'That you, Charles? Glad to hear from you. I'm busy now, but I'll be in touch when I get a chance – only don't refuse my message this time, will you?'

That was all. 'Wait a minute,' cried Forrester. 'Taiko!'

The joymaker interrupted him. 'Man Forrester, that was a recording.'

Forrester growled profanely. He walked around the office, examining it, but without finding anything that would help him locate Taiko. 'Well, hell,' he said. 'Let's see. Is anybody else I know still alive?'

'Man Forrester, Edwardino Wry is also ambient. Do you consider that he is known to you?'

'I doubt it, because I never heard of the son— Wait a minute. Was he one of the ones that beat me up?'

'Yes, Man Forrester.'

'Well, I don't want to see *him*. Forget it, joymaker,' said Forrester. 'I guess I'll just wait for Taiko.'

Three or four times he thought he saw people, but he was only able to get close to one of them, and it said civilly. 'We are not human, Man Forrester. We are merely a special purpose service unit diverted to aid at the cryogenic facilities.' It had looked like a pretty young blonde in a bikini, perhaps a barmaid somewhere, Forrester thought; but was too dispirited to inquire further. Apart from those, there was no one in sight in Shoggo.

He walked aimlessly, shaking his head.

His long days of self-imposed exile had let most of the guilt evaporate from him. He no longer felt either fearful of discovery or humiliated; the Sirian had used him as a tool, true, but if it had not been him, it would have been someone else. Anyway, he was more concerned about this world. The year 2527 was a great disappointment to him. He could think of no other age when the response of the populace to a threat of death would have been such universal suicide. It was simply crazy . . .

Of course, he reminded himself, death was not the same to these people as it had been to his contemporaries. Death was no longer necessarily permanent. It was like fleeing to a neutral country to sit out a war, and heaven knew there were lots of twentieth-century examples of that.

Nevertheless, in Charles Forrester's opinion the world of A.D. 2527 was chicken.

Forrester filled his lungs and shouted, 'You are all cowards! The world's better off without you!' His voice echoed emptily among the tall, hard building faces.

'Man Forrester,' said the joymaker, 'were you addressing me?'

'I was not. Shut up,' said Forrester. 'No, cancel that. Get

166

me a cab.' And, when it came, he took it back to the broad hovercraft way where he and Jerry Whitlow had hidden out as two of the Forgotten Men. But there were no more Forgotten Men in evidence, not wherever he looked, no matter how loudly he called out. 'Take me to Adne Bensen's home,' he commanded, and the cab flew him into the entrance port at the midtower level of the building they had shared, but there was no one visible there. Not in the streets, not in the halls, not even in the apartment, after Forrester had commanded the joymaker to let him in.

He ordered himself a meal and sat on the edge of a sort of couch in the children's room, feeling put-upon and sad. When he had finished eating he said, 'Joymaker, try getting Taiko for me again.'

'Yes, Man Forrester ... There is no new message, Man Forrester.'

'Don't give me that! Say it's priority, like you're always doing to me.'

'You do not have the authority to classify a message priority, Man Forrester.'

'I do if I say I'm planning to kill him,' Forrester said cunningly. 'You have to notify him of my intentions, right?'

'I do indeed, Man Forrester, but not until you have filed appropriate bonds and guaranties. Until you have done so, your notice cannot be effective. Do you wish to file, Man Forrester?'

'Well,' said Forrester, thinking about filling out forms and signing documents, 'I guess not, no. Isn't there *any* way I can get through to him?'

The joymaker said, 'I have a taped message from him, which I can display on the view-wall if you wish, Man Forrester. It is not, however, directly addressed to you.'

'Display the son of a gun then,' ordered Forrester. 'And make it snappy!'

'Yes, Man Forrester.'

The view-wall lighted up, obediently; but what appeared on it was not Taiko Hironibi. It was a tall, largely built woman with a commanding presence, who said, 'Girl Goldi-locks and Terror of Bears!'

The joymaker said apologetically, 'There is a malfunc-tion, Man Forrester. I am investigating.'

Forrester was startled. 'What the devil!' he cried. The voice went on. 'Bears! Think of bears. Great biting crea-tures, shaggy-haired, smell of animal sweat and rot. A bear can kill a man – *crunch*, crush his head; *smash*, crash his spine; *zip*, rip his heart.' At every word the woman's image acted out crunching, smashing, ripping.

'Hey,' said Forrester, 'I didn't order any bedtime stories!'

The joymaker said, in the same tone of apology, 'Man Forrester, the technical difficulty is being analyzed. I suggest you permit this tape to finish.'

And meanwhile the woman was orating.. 'A girl child, little as you. Littler. Little as you used to be when you were little. Call the girl . . . give her a name . . . Let her be called, oh, Goldilocks. Golden hair; locks of gold. Sweet, small, defenseless girl.'

Forrester snarled, 'Will you turn this damn thing *off*?'

'Man Forrester,' admitted the joymaker, 'I can't. Please be patient.'

'Imagine this girl doing a naughty thing!' cried the woman. 'Imagine her going where she should not go, where her mother/father told her not to go. Imagine her rejecting their wise counsel!'

Forrester sank back on the couch and said glumly, 'If you can't turn it off, at least get me a drink while I'm waiting. Scotch and water.'

'Yes, Man Forrester.'

The view-wall was showing real bears now, large and ferocious grizzlies, while the woman chanted, 'And Goldilocks goes to the bear lair – roaring, biting, slashing bears! But they are not home.

'They are not home, and she eats their food. She sits where they sit, lies where they lie, and sleeps.

'She sleeps, and the bears come home!'

Forrester's drink appeared; he tasted it and glowered, for it was not Scotch. As best as he could tell from the flavor, it was a sort of salty applejack.

'The bears come home! The bears come home, and their muzzles foam; the bears come back ready to attack, the bears come in with their jaws agrin!

'Red eyes glowing! (She sleeps, unknowing.)

'Claws that rend (is this the end?), paws that break (she starts to wake), teeth that bite—

'And Goldilocks opens her eyes, screams loudly, leaps to her feet and takes flight.'

The woman on the view-wall paused, staring sorrowfully straight into Forrester's eyes. Her oratorial stance relaxed; her eyes seemed to lose their dramatic glow, and she said conversationally, 'Now, you see? What a terrible thing to happen to a little girl, and all because she rejected her parents. She ran and ran and ran and ran, a long, long time, and then she got back to her father/mother and promised never to reject them again, and made a good adjustment. Now please prepare to answer questions on the theme: "Is it wise to take chances on going to places your father/mother do not approve?" ' She smiled, bowed, and vanished.

The joymaker said, 'Man Forrester, thank you for waiting. There are certain nexial recursions malfunctioning at the present time, and we regret any inconvenience.'

'What was that? One of Adne's kids' bedtime stories?'

'Exactly, Man Forrester. Our apologies. Shall I attempt to display the Taiko tape again?'

'I think,' said Forrester, with a sense of foreboding, 'that I am beginning to feel kind of lonesome.'

'That is not due to any malfunction on our part, Man Forrester,' said the joymaker with dignity. 'That is due to—'

Silence.

'What did you say?' demanded Forrester.

'That is due to— That is due to— *Awk*,' said the joymager, as thought it were strangling. 'That is due to the flight of many persons to freezing facilities.'

'You sound as though you're breaking down, machine,' said Forrester apprehensively.

'No, Man Forrester! Certain nexial recursions are not operative, and some algorithms are looping. It is a minor technical difficulty.'

The machine paused, then said in a different tone, 'Another minor technical difficulty is that certain priority programs have not been executed on schedule. My apologies, Man Forrester.'

'For what?'

'For not delivering a priority notice regarding your imminent arrest.'

Forrester was jolted. 'The devil you say!'

'No, Man Forrester. It is a true message. The coppers are coming for you now.'

SEVENTEEN

The door opened with a *thwack,* and two coppers plunged into the room. One of them grabbed him, rather roughly, Forrester thought, and glared into his eyes. 'Man Forrester!' it cried. 'You are arrested on sufficient charges and need make no statement!'

As if he could, thought Forrester, whirled off his feet as the coppers flanked him, one on each side, and half carried him out into the corridor and down to the fly-in, where a police flier was waiting for him. He shouted to them, 'Wait! What's it all about?'

They did not answer, merely thrust him in and slammed the door. It must be the Sirian business, he thought sickly, staring back at them as they watched the flier bear him away. But why now? 'I didn't *do* anything!' he cried knowing that he lied.

'That is to be determined, Man Forrester,' said a voice from a speaker grille over his head. 'Meanwhile, please come with us.'

The 'please' was totally sense-free, of course; Forrester had no choice. 'But what did I *do*?' he begged.

'Your arrest has been ordered, Man Forrester,' said the quiet, unemotional voice of the central computation facility. 'Do you wish a precis of the charge against you?'

'You bet!' Forrester stared around fearfully. There was no one at the controls, but there didn't seem to be a need for anyone; the car was sliding rapidly through the air toward the lake front.

'Your arrest has been ordered, Man Forrester,' repeated the computer voice. 'Do you wish a precis of the charge against you?'

'Damn it, I just said I did!' They were over blue water and

moving fast. Forrester hammered the fleshy part of his fist
against a window experimentally, but naturally enough the
glass did not break. It was just as well, of course; there was
no place for him to go.

'Your arrest,' said the computer voice calmly, 'has been
ordered, Man Forrester. Do you wish a precis of the charge
against you?'

Forrester swore furiously and hopelessly. They were
approaching a metal island in the lake, and the aircraft was
dropping toward it. 'All I want,' he said, 'is to know what
the devil's going on. Joymaker! Can you tell me what this is
all about?' But the mace clipped to his belt only said, 'We
are all the same, Man Forrester. Do you wish a precis of the
charge against you?'

By the time the aircraft landed, Forrester had regained
control of himself. Obviously something was wrong with the
central computation facilities, but equally obviously there
was nothing much he could do about it now. When two
more coppers, waiting on the hardstand for the police car to
alight, seized his arms and pulled him out of the door, he did
not resist. The coppers' grip was quite unbreakable, their
strength far greater than his own.

He saw no human being and no other automata, while he
was herded like livestock down through underground
passages, under the lake water, until finally he was pushed
into a door that locked behind him.

He was in a cell. It held a bed, a chair, and a table, nothing
else. Or nothing that was visible; its walls were mined with
the usual electronic maze, however, because a voice said at
once, 'Man Forrester, message.'

'Drop sick,' said Forrester. 'No, I don't want a precis of
the charge against me.'

But the message that followed was not the repetitious
drone of the faulty machines. It was Taiko's voice, and a
wall of the cell sprang into light to show his face. 'Hi, there,
Chuck,' he said. 'You said you wanted to see me.'

Forrester exhaled sharply. 'Thank God,' he said 'Look,

172

Taiko, something's gone wrong with the machines, and I'm in jail!'

Taiko's bland face creased in a smile. 'Number one,' he said, 'there's nothing wrong with the machines – in fact, something's going right with them! And, number two, of course you're in jail. Who do you think brought you here?'

'Here? You mean you're—'

Taiko grinned and nodded. 'Not more'n fifty meters away, pal. Considering how messed up the computers are, the easiest way to get you here was to have you arrested. So I did. So now we come right down to it, Are you with the Ned Lud Society or are you against it? Because this is our chance. Everything's so stirred up for fear of a Sirian invasion that we can straighten things out the *right* way. Know what I mean by the right way?'

'Smash the machines?' Forrester guessed. 'You mean, you and I are going to break up the central computers?'

'Oh, not just you and I,' said Taiko triumphantly. 'We've got a lot of help we didn't have before. Would you like to see them?'

Taiko touched his joymaker, and the field of the viewscreen widened. Forrester was looking into a fairly large room and a rather heavily populated one.

Taiko did indeed have a lot of help. There were perhaps a dozen of them, Forrester saw, but he did not count them very accurately. He was too shocked to count when he discovered that only one or two of the dozen 'helpers' in the room were human.

The rest were not. They looked out at Forrester through eyes that were circlets of gleaming green dots. They were Sirians.

'You see, pal,' said Taiko easily, 'it's a matter of loyalties. Our friends here are kind of funny-looking, I admit. But they're *organic*.'

Forrester goggled. The Sirians in their cone-shaped pressure suits looked exactly like his late friend and benefactor, S Four. The idea of making allies of them was hard to

173

accept. Not only because they were potentially dangerous enemies, but because his own contact with S Four had left him with an unshakable conviction that men and Sirians were far from being able to communicate on any meaningful level.

Taiko laughed. 'Takes you back, eh? But it was obvious – only it took somebody like me to see how to make it work. These guys are *geniuses* on the electronic stuff, absolute geniuses. They've given us a chance to put the ideals of the Ned Lud Society into practice, once and for all . . . Look, are you interested or not? Because I can send you back where you came from as easily as I brought you here.'

'I'm interested, all right,' said Forrester.

Taiko was sharp enough to catch a hint of double meaning. 'Interested to work with us? Or to try to mess us up?' But he didn't wait for an answer. He chuckled. 'Makes no difference in the long run,' he said merrily. 'What can you do? Come on up and talk it over, anyway . . .'

And there was a faint click, and the door of Forrester's cell sprang open, and a line of pale glowing green arrowheads appeared to point the way for him to walk.

I wish, he thought, that Adne were here to talk to.

But Adne was deep in the liquid-helium sleep of death, with her children, with nearly everyone else Forrester had met in this century. There was no one to tell him what to do.

He followed the tick of the arrowheads appearing before him as precisely as though they were the measures of a dance. It could not possibly be right, he told himself, to change the ways of the world with the aid of creatures from another star. It violated every principle of equity and human rights.

On the other hand, what Taiko was after made sense. Was it right to submit the destinies of the world to a cluster of computers?

For that matter, thought Forrester, tardily realizing how little of his homework he had done, was the premise right in

174

that statement? *Were* the computers masters of the world? Who *did* make fundamental decisions?

Was it possible that a state had been reached in which fundamental decisions made themselves – not by the acts of a legislature, but by the actions of sovereign individuals, viewed en masse?

He shook his head. It was rather pointless to be considering these large questions, in view of his circumstances. He was several hundred meters under the surface of a lake, he reminded himself, in a world that had rejected him several times and was now dissolving around him.

The arrowheads ended at a door, which wheeled itself open as he approached, and he entered the room he had seen in the view-screen.

'About time!' cried Taiko, advancing toward him and clapping him on the shoulder. 'You know, Charles, you should have confided in me. If it hadn't been for my friends here—' he gestured at the Sirians in their conical suits – 'I'd never have known how much you had to do with our success. Haw! You *said* you'd help the society if I'd let you join. I just had no idea how much!'

'So you know how S Four tricked me,' said Forrester.

'Don't be modest! It was a noble deed – even if he had to, well, lean on you a little to make you do it. I can only wonder,' Taiko went on modestly, 'why I didn't think of it myself. Obviously, the way to make Ned Lud ideals real is to get enough people so chicken-scared that they light out for the freezers, leaving the rest of the world to take care of whatever happens next. Only there isn't enough rest of the world still alive to matter. And while things are messed up, we *move*.'

One of the Sirians moved restlessly. Its circlet of green eyes winked like gems, dimmed only faintly by the sheen of the crystal band that kept it from the corrosive attack of Earth's air. It did not speak, but Taiko seemed to understand what it was thinking.

'They don't exactly want you here,' he said, turning a

thumb toward the Sirian. 'Not that they're not grateful. Well, whatever a Sirian would be that you might call grateful. But there's a lot riding on all this for them, and they don't like to take chances.'

'Do you want me to promise not to interfere?' asked Forrester wonderingly.

'No! Who'd believe you'd keep a promise like that? Anyway, it isn't necessary. What could you do?'

'I don't know.'

'Nothing! We've already recircuited most of Central Computation – no communication anywhere, anymore. Except for the coppers – which are under our direct control – and the DR vehicles. Which I insisted on,' he pointed out, 'because naturally I'm not going to *hurt* any human beings if I can help it. Sweat! I want to *save* them!'

'What about your friends here?'

'Forget them, Charles,' said Taiko easily. 'Don't fret yourself, they're just technical advisors. I'm the one that's running this show, and when we finish busting up the machines they're going home.'

'How do you know?' Forrester damanded.

'Oh, sweat, Charles,' sighed Taiko. He glanced ruefully at the Sirians, shook his head, took Forrester by the arm. He walked him over to a view-wall and pointed.

'The pictures are a little random and fuzzy,' he apologized, 'because naturally Central Computing isn't monitoring the intercuts any more. But look. You see what the world looks like now?'

Forrester looked. One wall showed a broad hoverway with a single car on it, lying slantwise across the way and motionless; no one was around. The other wall changed as he watched from blank gray to a growing fire that seemed to be consuming most of the central part of a city. It did not look like Shoggo.

'You think the Sirians are going to worry about Earth without Central Computing?' demanded Taiko. 'Sweat, no! Once the machine computation facilities are neutralized, they'll be glad to go home. Earth won't be a threat. And they're not naturally warlike.'

'How do you know that?'

'Oh, come on, Charles! You have to take *some* things on faith!'

Forrester said carefully, 'Are you all that good a judge of Sirian character? Please, I'm not trying to put you down. I want to know. How can you be sure?'

'It stands to reason!' snapped Taiko. 'Oh, I know, Charles, you're thinking of the way I've been acting, like a clown, an idiot, pushing an idea that not one human being in a hundred thousand gave a hoot about, warning about dangers most people thought were delights ... But I'm not stupid. I moved in fast enough when you gave me the break, right? I showed I was smart enough to grab a chance when it presented itself? So trust me. I'm smart enough to see that there's nothing in it for the Sirians as far as fighting Earth is concerned. Why would they want to do that? They can't live here without suits. There are a thousand planets that would be worth something to them; Earth doesn't happen to be one of them.'

There was a sound from the voice-box of one of the Sirians. Taiko jumped. He turned to call out, 'All right, just a minute.' And, to Forrester, 'Well, that's it. I'm a sentimental slob. I'd like to have you with us since you did us a favor – whether you knew it or not. But it's up to you. In or out?'

'I don't know,' said Forrester honestly.

'Take your time,' grinned Taiko. 'The jail's yours. Just remember, there's nothing you can do to hurt us. No communications. No transportation. And damn near *nobody*.'

Forrester walked back out into the bright, empty corridors of Shoggo's underwater jail. No one stopped him.

There were no green arrows to guide him. As he had come from the left, he turned to the right. He wanted to think. Was Taiko right? Judging from his own experience, this was at least a disconcerting society, filled with unexpected

x

177

cruelties and cowardices. But who was Taiko to make the world's decisions for it?

He saw a bright light ahead and walked toward it. It was sunlight shining down a shaft, and a white death-reversal car humming quietly to itself as it waited.

There was an attendant, but though it looked human enough it glared into Forrester's eyes and said challengingly, 'Man Forrester! Your arrest has been ordered. Do you wish a precis of the charge against you?'

'Machine,' he said, 'you're a broken record.' Then he had a thought. 'Take me out of here!' he commanded, climbing into the DR flier.

'Man Forrester! Your arrest has been ordered. Do you wish a precis of the charge against you?'

It was hopeless, of course. He hoped, anyway, and sat there for minutes, while the machine that looked so like a human being glared unmovingly at him and the DR car remained motionless. Then Forrester sighed, got out, walked away.

'I might as well join them,' he said aloud.

But he didn't want to. He didn't merely not want to; he actively, passionately wished he could thwart Taiko's plan. As soon as it became clear he had only one choice to make, that choice became abhorrent.

But there was nothing he could do. He considered possibilities, one by one. Nothing would work. His joymaker was mute. There was no way out of the jail. Even the DR car would take him away only if he were dead, not alive . . .

If he were dead??

He took a deep breath and marched back to the DR car. As he had thought, the side of it was emblazoned with the caduceus of the WEST ANNEX CENTER.

He demanded, 'Machine, are you really operating out of the West Annex Center?'

The robot glared into his eyes. 'Man Forrester! Your arrest has been ordered. Would you like a precis of the charge against you?'

178

'What I would like,' said Forrester tightly, 'is an insurance policy. But I guess I'll have to take a chance this one time without one. Let's hope it's only your speaking circuits that are messed up!'

What he wanted he knew he would find in the flier. He reached into it, fumbled through the nest of first-aid equipment.

The thing he wanted turned up in the first case he opened: a four-inch scalpel, razor sharp. He stared at it glumly, hesitated, searched again until he found a writing stylus and a square of cardboard. Carefully he lettered a sign:

REVIVE ME AT ONCE!
I can tell you what the Sirians are up to.

He pinned it neatly to his shirt front. Then . . .

'Machine!' he cried. 'Do your duty!' And with a rapid motion he slit his throat.

The pain was astonishing, but it lasted for only a moment. And then the world roared thinly at him and slipped dizzyingly away.

EIGHTEEN

'I was dreaming,' murmured Forrester into the warm, comfortable darkness, 'of committing suicide. Funny I should cut my throat, though. I want to live . . .'

'You'll live, Chuck,' said a familiar voice. Forrester opened his eyes and gazed into the eyes of Hara.

He thrust himself up. 'Taiko!' he cried. 'The Sirians! I've got to tell you what they're doing!'

Hara pressed him back down on the bed. 'You already told us, Chuck. They're taken care of. Don't you remember?'

'Remember?' But then he did remember. He remembered being awake, with a nightmarish pain in his throat, trying by gesture and sign language to communicate something, until at last someone had had the wit to bring stylus and paper and he'd written out a message. He laughed out loud. 'Funny! I never thought that with my throat cut it'd be hard to tell you anything.'

'But you did, Chuck. The Sirians are under personal human guard, every one of them immobilized and cut off from communication. And Taiko's talking as fast as he can to a computer team, telling them what he did so they can undo it. They've already got all the basic utilities back.' Hara stood up, fished in a pocket, proudly produced a pack of cigarettes. 'Here,' he said. 'See how your new throat lining stands up to these.'

Forrester gratefully accepted a light. It felt all right as he drew in; he reached up and touched his throat, found it covered with soft plastic film.

'That'll come off today,' said Hara. 'You're about ready to go back to population. We've already revived close to twenty-five percent of the recent freezees. They'll really be interested in you.'

'Oh,' said Forrester, dampened. 'I guess they will, at that. What's the penalty for letting the Sirian escape?'

'About equal to the reward for letting us know about Taiko,' said Hara cheerfully. 'Don't worry about it.'

'Well, how about if I worry about what the Sirians are going to do?' asked Forrester.

Hara waved a hand. 'Be my guest,' he said. 'Only bear in mind that Taiko's little friends were pretty high when he was dismantling Central Computation, and they're pretty low now. I don't think they'll find us an easy target.'

He turned toward the door. 'Get yourself checked out,' he ordered. 'Then I want to talk to you before you leave here.'

'About my throat?'

'About your girl,' said Hara.

Hours later, Forrester was standing where he had stood before, outside the main entrance to the West Annex Discharge Center. For old time's sake he flipped a cigarette to the ground and watched the tiny bright cleaner robot whisk it up and away.

Clearly, Central Computation was back on the job.

He turned as Hara joined him. 'What *about* my girl?' he demanded.

'Well . . .' Hara hesitated. 'It's tough to know how to talk to you survivors of the kamikaze era,' he said. 'You're sensitive about the strangest things. For instance, Adne said she thought you resented the fact that I was the father of one of her kids.'

'*One* of them!' Forrester squawked, severely trying his new throat lining. 'Holy God! I at least thought they'd have the same father!'

'Why, Chuck?'

'Why? What do you mean, why? The girl's a trollop!'

'What's a trollop?' As Forrester hesitated, Hara pressed

181

on. 'In *your* time, maybe that was something bad. I don't know; I'm not a specialist in ancient history. But you aren't in your time anymore, Chuck.'

Forrester gazed thoughtfully at Hara's patient, weary face. But it was more than he wanted to accept. 'I don't care,' he said angrily. 'I can't help thinking maybe Taiko was right. Somewhere the human race took a wrong turning!'

'Well,' said Hara, 'actually, that's what I wanted to tell you. Chuck, there's no such thing as a wrong turning. You can't rewrite the history of the race; it happened; this is the result. If you don't like it, there's no reason why you can't try to persuade the world to change again. To something different – anything! Whatever you like. But *you can't go back.*'

He patted Forrester's shoulder. 'Think,' he advised. 'Let your brain decide what's right and wrong, not what's left of your boyhood training. Because all that is dead ... And, oh yes. One other thing,' he mentioned. 'I checked the schedules. We're reviving them pretty fast now, and it ought to be Adne's turn in about two days.'

And he was gone.

Forrester stared after him. It would be hard, he thought, but it would be possible. And, after all, he had very little choice.

So Forrester hailed a flier and ordered it to take him to a suitable dwelling in Shoggo, determined to face the future. Which, as it turned out, was very fortunate, since he had a lot of future to face – not just a few days or years, but, with the help of a few more visits to the freezer, a fair number of millennia, in all of which he was alive, and active, and well.

For he lived happily ever after. And so did they all.

Author's Note

Once upon a time, a quarter of a century or so ago, I was a weatherman for the United States Army Air Force in Italy. It was my first experience in the art of predicting real-time events – that is, in the kind of prediction where money, and lives, are bet on its accuracy.

This was a long time before the advent of the computer and the facsimile machine and TIROS and all the other handy little gadgets that have since come reasonably close to turning meteorology into an exact science. Still, we had our gadgets even then, quite a few of them. Our group weather officer, in my part of the Fifteenth Air Force, was a disheveled captain who smiled and nodded a lot, but rarely spoke. He would hum to himself for an hour or two as he pored over the teletype reports and the synoptic map and the adiabatic charts and the PIREPS. Then he would go out to the instrument shelter and swing the psychrometer and tap the aneroid barograph with his fingernail. And then he would climb on the roof of the station and perhaps he would see, off on the horizon, a cloud no bigger than a man's hand; and he would say, 'Ha! Looks like rain,' and come back and make a bad-weather forecast for the pilots of the B-24s.

Actually, that's the way to write science fiction. (Well, one kind of science fiction. There are many varieties of the science fiction experience!) First you do your homework with the books and the scientific journals. Then you talk to the astronomers and biochemists and computer people, and if you're lucky perhaps they'll let you play with their machines and look through their lenses. And then you get up on a high place and look at the world around you.

The Age of the Pussyfoot *was constructed to those specifications. Little of it represents invention on my part,* barring the personalities and some of the details of settings and events. Almost every aspect of it is visible right now, in July of 1968, as a cloud no bigger than a man's hand; and I too am forecasting rain.

The joymaker? M.I.T.'s Project MAC was what made me think of the joymaker – well, that's not quite true; I had thought of it before Project MAC ever existed, but certainly MAC is a sort of Jurassic ancestor of my toy. At M.I.T., two big IBM 7094s, plus half a dozen or so servant computers, are available to anyone with a remote-access console in his home or office. The console right now can be anywhere a telephone line will go – including Europe, if you like, or for that matter Antarctica. My only additional assumption is that it will be convenient to do the same thing by radio. The MAC consoles are presently about the size of biggish electric typewriters; my only change involved micro-miniaturizing them into portability – and, while you're at it, fitting them with a few of such necessities of modern urban life as Miltown, contraceptive pills, aspirin, and the like. I also assume that the pharmacopeia of the next few centuries will be more extensive than our own, but that seems like a reasonably good bet.

Immortality through freezing? Robert C. W. Ettinger has been on a crusade for that for more than five years now. The funny thing about it is that it will probably work. (I offer no money-back guarantees, you understand, only an opinion. But it is an opinion shared by such prestigious men as Jean Rostand, France's most illustrious biochemist.) The other funny thing about it is that there have been very few takers for this offer of immortality in the flesh – as Bob Ettinger says, many are cold, but few are frozen. There are fewer than half a dozen corpses currently in the deep freeze, although there are some hundreds of thousands of persons who would be, except that they haven't yet happened to die. But the facilities are there, including some three competing lines of the man-sized thermos bottles with the liquid-gas tanks that are now commercially available for those who

184

would die and live to die again. I mentioned 'death-reversal' equipment in the story. Several years ago, I saw an unpublished manuscript that stated, apparently on good authority, that the U.S.S.R. had such vehicles in service then; it implied that one of these had saved the life of the noted Russian scientist Lev Landau. (Who was dead four times, clinically, incontrovertibly dead, before he was brought to life again permanently enough to be released from the hospital.) And, three months ago, parked outside the headquarters of the New York Academy of Sciences, I saw the first American death-reversal machine. The New York DR vehicle is a truck; those in the story are helicopters. Otherwise they are much the same.

It is true, however, that no corpsicle has yet been thawed and returned to life, and there's no firm estimate of when one will be. Yet it could happen tomorrow. The odds appear to be very great that it will happen some time, and according to my personal reading of human psychology, the minute it does we will have a rush to the freezers comparable to no human migration since the opening of the Cherokee Strip. It strikes me that we are all, from birth, so often reminded that we are inevitably going to die that we cannot accept an offer of immortality when it is presented, until and unless it is shown to work. Demonstrate that it works one time, and we'll grab for it as we've grabbed for few things before ... and then the building of such installations as the West Annex Center will proceed apace.

The economic, social, and cultural 'predictions' of the story are perhaps a little less defensible than the hardware. But I think the reason for that is that economics and sociology, et al., are at the present time rather less 'scientific' than the hard sciences are. The money part of the story is pretty reliably stated. Obviously we will continue to have both of the two kinds of inflation that have been going on throughout history – both the devaluation of existing currencies (as the Roman solidus, worth several hundred dollars at least, was devalued over two thousand years into the French sou, worth not even a thank you); and the multiplication of things to spend money on, which is the psychological root of a good deal of the 'poverty' of our own age and nation. (America's poor usually do have enough money to survive on. I is the fact that they see around them so many desirable things, which they don't have money to buy, that makes them really, miserably, unarguably 'poor'.)

The notion of being paid a salary for things we might now consider to be properly unpaid, leisure-time activities is no particularly fanciful, either. Witness the proposals of the guaranteed annual wage and the negative income tax witness institutionalized welfare programs; witness how many 'leisure' activities have already become paying professions. Who would have paid a salary to a ski instructor in the Middle Ages? Already in America almost every large volunteer organization has a hard-core paid professional staff. (It is not quite as common in Europe – yet.) I am only suggesting that the memberships as well as the leadership might as well be paid for what they do.

As to the mating customs, the interpersonal folkways and so on of my twenty-sixth-century characters, I confess I am on shakier ground. I am not sure that things will go exactly this way. But form follows function. There is a need for a family even now, as a sort of nest designed for the raising of children, and there no doubt will be such a need in the foreseeable future. I do not think it will be the same need as in the recent past, however. Then there was enough work at home to keep an able-bodied woman busy from dawn to dark, and enough work involved in earning a living to keep her husband away at the farm or factory almost every waking hour. With the increase in leisure time, in productivity of labor, especially in such external aids to child-rearing as schools and nurseries, the functional need for the family is somewhat different. Our social structure has not yet really caught up with that fact, although the signs are writ large; am only assuming that in five hundred years it will have done so.

A similar defense could be made for almost every speculation in this novel, including the presence of Sirians. (Or, anyway, extraterrestrial creatures capable of doing the sort of thing that Sirians do in the story. There are more than one hundred billion stars in our own galaxy, and it is a dead-certain bet that at least some of them have inhabited planets.) But I should confess that there are two areas in which I am defenseless.

One of these includes the things I have left out. I have not taken into consideration the probabilities of large-scale disaster — through nuclear warfare, or lethal pollution of the air, or a runaway population explosion sufficient to starve us all back to the Neolithic. But there's just so much you can discuss in one story, and I wasn't happening to discuss those possibilities here.

And the other thing I can't defend is the time scale.

If you put together Project MAC and Bob Ettinger's freezers and the negative income tax, you have something that is really quite a lot like The Age of the Pussyfoot ... *constructed out of materials that are to hand right now. In the novel, the time scale is large: five centuries. Charles Forrester's revival is as far in one direction along our time scale as Christopher Columbus's voyage is in the other.*

I don't really think it will be that long. Not five centuries. Perhaps not even five decades.

FREDERIK POHL
Red Bank, New Jersey
July 1968

187